wide brown land

wide brown land

stories of titan

simon petrie

First published in Australia in 2018

Please direct all enquiries to the publisher at:
fomalhaut451@gmail.com

ISBN 978-0-6483228-2-5

Typeset in Adobe Garamond Pro / Candara
Cover photograph by derumka / Shutterstock
Cover artwork and internal illustrations by Shauna O'Meara

National Library of Australia Cataloguing-in-Publication entry

Title: Wide Brown Land: stories of Titan / Simon Petrie.
ISBN: 9780648322825 (pbk.)
Subjects: Science fiction, Australian.
              Short stories, Australian.
Other Authors / Contributors:
              Harvey, Edwina, editor.
              O'Meara, Shauna, illustrator.
Dewey Number: A823.4

table of contents

books by simon petrie

(the titan sequence)
Matters Arising from the Identification of the Body
Wide Brown Land
A Reappraisal of the Circumstances Resulting in Death (forthcoming)

Flight 404
Murder on the Zenith Express: the Gordon Mamon collection
80,000 Totally Secure Passwords That No Hacker Would Ever Guess

to murray, colin, and peter

who presumably would not have imagined
that it would come to this

preface

When I started to fancy myself a writer of fiction, and more particularly a writer of hard SF, it was natural that, ultimately, Titan would get a look-in. I've had a fascination with – some would probably say a fixation on – Saturn's smog moon Titan for the past three decades now, starting with my days as a callow PhD student at the University of Canterbury in New Zealand. The atmospheric chemistry of Titan wasn't entirely relevant to my research in interstellar cloud chemistry, but it wasn't exactly not relevant either; and I think I have my PhD supervisor, Murray McEwan, to thank for planting in my mind the seed of an interest in the formation of carbon-containing molecules in Titan's ionosphere.

It was more than a decade after my PhD before I would turn my hand to investigating Titan's atmospheric chemistry in any significant sense. My first effort in this direction, undertaken at the Australian National University, was a study[1] advancing the hypothesis that hydrogen isocyanide, HNC (a vicious and disagreeable compound known to be a significant trace constituent of carbon-rich interstellar clouds) ought to be, by virtue of chemical processes similar to those occurring in IS clouds, detectable by spectroscopic means in the upper reaches of Titan's atmosphere. A second study,[2] so speculative that it might inadvertently qualify as fiction, involved the chemical fate of infalling meteoric material in Titan's upper atmosphere;

---

1   *Icarus* **151** (2001) 196.
2   *Icarus* **171** (2004) 199

a third study, a pigeon-pair collaborative effort with the Japanese theoretical chemist Yoshihiro Osamura,[3] explored the hypothesis that existing models of titanian atmospheric chemistry employed intrinsically inefficient and likely non-viable pathways to the production of the known constituents dicyanogen and dicyanoacetylene,[4] NCCN and NCCCCN respectively, and proposed instead a new network of reactions involving the then-still-hypothetical titanian molecule HNC (see above) to account for the observed abundances of NCCN and NCCCCN. That, in capsule form, is the sum total of my contribution to human knowledge of the atmospheric chemistry of Titan; such is the incremental pace in the advancement of science.

You probably don't need to know, but I'll tell you anyway, that a team of radioastronomers from France, Germany, Poland and Spain subsequently reported[5] a positive detection of HNC in Titan's atmosphere, an outcome which, in stoic scientific parlance, I consider to be 'a hit, a palpable hit!' As to the reliability of my other supposedly non-fictional offerings on Titan, the jury is still out... which is, more or less, how these things go. One can only be cautiously presumed correct until one is proven wrong.

Then the fiction happened. I wrote a story called 'Shitstorm' in the first months of 2009. After passage through the Canberra Speculative Fiction Guild (CSFG) short story critiquing group, it underwent a name change to 'Storm in a T-Suit', and that's the title it appeared under, in 2010, in *Aurealis* 44. As a story which was, in large part, pantsed, it's proved remarkably formative for me, and it would seem that I have not stopped writing Titan stories yet.

I should foreshadow that, though there are consciously-placed links between several of these stories, with recurring characters and some contingencies of plot, they do not neatly construct a single larger story. In particular, they do not continue the thread of conceptual SF

---

3   Osamura & Petrie, *J. Phys. Chem. A* **108** (2004) 3613; Petrie & Osamura, *J. Phys. Chem. A* **108** (2004) 3623.

4   The prefix here is 'di-', not 'dicy-', knowledge of which may prove useful towards the correct pronunciation of those names.

5   Moreno et al, *Astron. Astrophys.* **536** (2011) L12.

extrapolation unreeled within 'Storm in a T-Suit' – and you will, I think, recognise to which thread I'm referring when you encounter it. There will be more on this elsewhere, but not here.

My guiding lights for these stories have been the books of authors like Arthur C Clarke and Kim Stanley Robinson: in books such as Clarke's *A Fall of Moondust* and *The Sands of Mars*, and Robinson's epic Mars trilogy, the focus is less on the longstanding SF tropes of bug-eyed monsters, derring-do in space, and travel through the Galaxy at impossible speeds, and more on a sober and immersive portrayal of what life might actually be like were we to venture a little further into our own fascinating neighbourhood. I hope, in these stories, I've been able to capture a sense of that 'sense of wonder', if on a smaller scale.

I also hope I've largely got it right. One of the dangers of writing near-future SF, even if it's middle-distance-near-future rather than immediate-vicinity-near-future, is that the extrapolation necessary to envisage what-might-be is soon overridden by what-becomes. For a subject such as future human colonisation of Titan, this applies both to the evolution of human society and its technology, and to our understanding of a cloud- and haze-shrouded extraterrestrial environment which has long seemed intent on guarding its secrets. Almost uniquely among the Solar System's moons, Titan cannot simply be mapped by high-resolution photography, which means we still know less about its topography than that of, say, Europa, or Enceladus, or perhaps even one face of Pluto. There's a strong sense, still, of 'here be dragons' in the latest maps of Titan, with large swathes remaining vague and uncharacterised – a situation which, in this immediate post-Cassini era, is not likely to change anytime soon. This is, of course, part of Titan's appeal as a setting, but it also makes it a hazardous backdrop against which to attempt hard SF. What's it actually like to delve beneath the surface of one of Titan's liquid-methane lakes? To experience a windstorm in a titanian environment? To traverse regions clogged by hydrocarbon sand? To come into direct contact with that thick, unbreathable, lethally cold atmosphere? We don't know, and I've been forced, repeatedly, to guess. This guesswork has always been a part of SF, but it's an intrinsically dodgy business. I've sought to minimise the risk through assiduous perusal of recent academic papers on titanian geography, meteorology, and geochemistry, and in this regard I'd particularly like to acknowledge the usefulness of the SAO / NASA Astrophysics Data System,[6] a freely-available service containing just about all the published research in astronomy and astrophysics: it's long been my standard go-to site for our aggregated knowledge on Titan. (For those without academic access, it's limited to abstracts rather than full papers in many cases, but you can still learn a lot from a well-written abstract.) I'm also very grateful to Dr Ralph D. Lorenz, of Johns Hopkins University's Applied Physics Lab, for his careful perusal of the manuscript and identification of several pieces of fallacious detail. Any residual errors in the following pages are, of course, my own responsibility.

It remains also to thank the various participants in the monthly CSFG crit groups through which these stories were fed, a process which certainly resulted in substantial improvement; and to express my continuing gratitude towards the editors of the outlets in which many of these stories first appeared (or, in one case, would have appeared if not for a late change in magazine policy regarding fiction). In alphabetical order, these brave souls are: Sam Bellotto Jr., Juliet Buchanan, Anna Caro, Cassie Hart, Edwina Harvey, Stuart Mayne, Cat Sparks, and Keith Stevenson. They are fine individuals, every one.

Finally, I am especially grateful to Shauna O'Meara for her wonderful cover art and interior artwork, and to the patient and incisive editing of Edwina Harvey.

Now: go! Turn the page! To Titan!

I hope it doesn't disappoint.

Simon Petrie
April 2018

---

6   http://adswww.harvard.edu

wide brown land

stories of titan

storm in a t-suit

Who in their right mind went out, voluntarily, into a Titanian shitstorm?

Cursing, Mats slewed the big quad-ski to a treacherous halt in a curve of brownsugar snow. He fired off a couple of anchorage harpoons for good measure. The downslope ahead would be difficult, would require negotiation on its own terms.

Get a grip, he told himself, as the memories threatened to subvert his resolve. *This is Titan, not the Valles Marineris. More than enough happening in the here and now.*

The old melanoma scar on Mats's forehead began to ache: fatigue, tension, frustration, a fair dollop of anger. Behind all else, foreboding. Not helped by the eyestrain of trying to navigate through *this*. Pausing at the top was as much a sanity break as it was an opportunity to gain a better vantage. But pause meant delay. And every moment of delay was another moment to fear for the safety of Mercedes, and the other two.

The valley ahead was sepulchral, a study in dun and orange, smothered by a hazy brown sky. Within the landscape, further features were vague, not helped by the adhesion of this groundblown crud to the quad-ski's windscreens, and to the visor of his own T-suit.

No sign of the rover, or its crew. But they'd come this way. He tried hailing them again, tried calling Leto too. Nothing. Out of range, or just too much junk in the atmosphere. Bad news either way.

He climbed out of the quad-ski's passenger cage, gripping a side support against the wind. The denser air-mass, weaker gravity: Titan didn't do hurricanes, nor anything remotely resembling, but a shitstorm gusting at up to twenty kilometres an hour could churn up plenty of material. Could prove deadly in its own right.

Mats knew deadly. Mats had been haunted for eighteen years by deadly.

The wind was a constant, low, note-bending growl. Its noise was overlaid by the *flack... flack... flack* of the larger flakes of crud as they landed on the visibility-blue shell of his T-suit. A glob like birdshit impacted wetly on his visor, and he instinctively wiped it aside with a sweep of his glove, leaving a worse mess.

He muttered *refresh*. The T-suit's storm visor obediently shucked off an ultrathin layer of film, affording him a momentarily improved view. Not that it helped overly, his eyesight wasn't what it had once been. He wondered how many visor-film layers were left, before he was reduced to the baseplate. Not that many. Not enough. His visor was yucking up again, already. Mats *hated* shitstorms.

He peered forward, looking to spy out the best approach down to the valley's floor, and spied something out of place. A smear of orange-green, near the slope's base. A clue. Another navigational challenge. It was difficult to be sure, but it looked like a trail marker.

Refresh. He looked again, and his breath snagged. It wasn't a trail marker.

Barely a hundred metres; but it took half an hour to manoeuvre the quad-ski down the slope to the T-suited figure. That was the easy part.

The figure lay sprawled face-down, concealing both its identity and the array of med telltales incorporated into the suit's chest display. There was no way of telling whether life yet remained within. And Mats's heart slumped further when he saw how firmly the once-blue T-suit had become wedded to the frozen surface. Heat from the suit's servoes, most likely, had caused the brine to melt in thin transient patches; that, and thermal leakage from a poorly-insulated helmet. Warmth had departed the suit like a spirit.

The rescue equipment he'd brought with him, from Leto, had been chosen for rover retrieval. The quad-ski was equipped for towing, and for reasonably heavy lifting. It would certainly be up to the task of pulling an occupied T-suit from the ground's cold grasp. But the T-suit itself wouldn't necessarily withstand the stresses involved. And there was nothing on board the quad-ski that was designed for excavation.

At least the suit was small. Joachim was tall. Mercedes was much shorter, but then so was Frank.

Mats didn't know what to hope for. Didn't wish to find his daughter dead; but the prolonged doubt was corrosive, took him all the way back to Mars. And this T-suit's occupant *was* small…

Torn by haste and caution, Mats stared at the figure before him, searching for a shortcut that he knew didn't exist. Turned to look at the quad-ski five metres away, hoping for reassurance from its workaday solidity. But the vehicle suddenly seemed a small, fragile thing, lost like him within planetary-scale vastness. Beneath the husk of his own T-suit, his ribcage tightened.

He shook himself. The time wasn't his to waste. The figure in front of him might well be Mercedes. He had a rescue to attempt.

He returned to the quad-ski, for one of the anchorage harpoons.

It took Mats a good forty minutes with the harpoon, forty minutes of stabbing at the dirty-glass crud entombing the figure, before he was ready to try levering it out. He'd paid particular attention to the region around the head of the T-suit. Not only had the adhesion been most extensive there, but he needed to ensure that there wasn't too much resistance, too much residual grip between the ground and the visor. If the visor remained cold-welded to the surface while the rest of the T-suit came free…

The first attempt didn't work. Mats could sense that the opposing vectors, his application of leverage against the ground's reluctance, were still too great for the T-suit to handle. So he set to once more, kneeling on the trammelled ice around the T-suit, his own suit's harsh headlamps drowning out the frail, storm-shielded light of the early-afternoon sun. He jammed the harpoon repeatedly into the broken ground, the action becoming mechanical, ritual, devoid of significance as it built its own rhythm.

He grew desperately tired, fearful that he'd slip with the harpoon, would pierce the T-suit through mischance or through mesmerized incaution. Every several minutes he stood, dizzy each time, each time having to fight to prise his lower legs up from the tar-like slush that, like an addict, sucked steadily at the warmth leaking from his own suit's knee servos.

His visor had gone beyond 'refresh' by the end, and he was working almost blind, trying to see through near-opacity. His suit's servoes, intended to compensate for the difficulty of stiff-suited manual exertion against Titan's ambient overpressure, had become sapped by cold to the extent that they were more encumbrance than assistance. And he'd reached the point where he was losing confidence in his ability to distinguish chopped-up Titanian gravel-slush from precious T-suited human meat. He pushed the harpoon as far under the figure as he dared, and heaved downwards.

The T-suit came free, encrusted with an encumbrance of coffee-stained syrupy muck. He turned the suit over. He still couldn't make out the idents, or discern the med telltales' status, but the suit's weight was sufficient identity of its occupant.

He stooped in preparation to pick her up, but the motion took on a life of its own. He sank to his knees, as something that had lain within him almost two decades struggled to emerge. The static in his ears grew deafening, threatened to overpower. He forced himself to breathe deep, slow, regular. To take the necessary steps.

At least, this time, there was a body.

He carried his daughter's body back to the quad-ski's passenger cage, strapped her as best he could into one of the front seats, and wiped her T-suit down. Then he plugged a cable from the vehicle's auxiliary heating unit into the jack at her suit's hip, and set about the task of emergency suit rehab.

The suit's med lights were off. Which was clearly very bad, spoke volumes about the length of time Mercedes had lain sprawled out there, seeping out precious body heat. But Mats was experienced enough to know that the status panels were designed to power down a little before the ultimate failure of the suit's life support, meaning that there was still some cruel hope. *Might* still be some hope. He'd know soon enough: there was a med-status recharge piggybacked onto the thermal conduit running from quad-ski to suit.

Her T-suit's backtank showed she was out of nutrients. Mats pulled a liquid-rations syringe out of the warmth of the quad-ski's first-aid locker, slipped its secure-seal needle through the septum on the upper compartment of the backtank. Strained to squeeze the crude nutrient mix through, his fingers' clumsiness amplified by the gloves. Slapped a thick gob of emergency sealant over the septum, once he'd withdrawn the needle. Queried her med telltales. Still no response. Not good. But at least she could feed, now, if she needed to.

The bodily-waste tank in the backtank's basal compartment appeared to be frozen through, which meant that extraction – basically the reverse of the nutrient-loading process – faced a delay. Another bad sign.

Finally, the first med light came on. Yellow.

For quite some time Mats did not trust himself to speak. It was Mercedes' voice, thin, uncertain, that emerged first.

'What was the expiry date on those rations?' she asked.

He didn't laugh, made no immediate response whatever. Then, 'Don't know what Frank thought he was playing at, three in a rover.

It's totally against regs.'

'That's how it had to be, Dad. I was there for the geochem, Joachim for navigation. Frank because… well, Frank…'

Beside him, she was quiet and so still that he thought she'd drifted into unconsciousness again, until he felt her gloved fingers gently squeezing his. 'You came from this way, right?' he asked, waving, indicating the view through the quad-ski's barely-translucent windscreen.

'Uh… yeah. The rover's trapped in a crevasse about three klicks due west of the thirty-five kay mark on the cargo track. There's a methane-ethane pond nearby, where Frank had been wanting to… but the radio wasn't…'

'Thirty-five kay?' he asked, a degree of surprise added to the question's inflection.

'It had to be me,' she answered. 'I had the most left in my tank.'

She had to have known the suit wasn't up to that level of endurance, not in these conditions. He was amazed she'd got as far back as she had. 'Joachim? Frank?' he asked.

'Frank's *dead*, Dad,' she replied. 'Joachim – but that was three days ago…'

He waited her out, tried fruitlessly to coax some life back into the quad-ski's radio, then busied himself with putting the vehicle through a wide, deliberate arc across the knurled landscape. The reorientation caught her notice, and it was with distinctly more animation, panic even, that she called out, 'What are you doing? We can't just leave him! I mean—'

'We're not leaving him,' he reassured. 'But if the rover's that distance away, and so close to the cargo track, then it makes sense to follow that rather than to attempt the whole way cross-country.'

Beside him, she was silent again. Eventually he discovered that she'd drifted back into sleep, or something akin.

The cargo track, worn almost smooth and packed down by the regular passage of the big cargo haulers, allowed Mats to open up the quad-ski's reserves of power, to put on more speed. It also afforded him more opportunity to monitor what was happening inside the vehicle, rather than outside. Mercedes' med telltales, relayed to the quad-ski's main console, kept shading intermittently from green into yellow, and her breathing was worryingly shallow and inconsistent. She drifted in and out of coherence; at times he'd hear a rapid sharp intake of breath, but could not tell whether this was grief – he knew she'd been close to Frank – or some more innately physiological damage.

'Madness, heading out into a shitstorm like this,' he commented eventually. 'What *did* Frank think he was playing at?'

'There was never any indication it was going to develop like this,' she argued. 'It started out as just a gentle browndown, and we all figured it would stay that way.'

'He should have known,' said Mats.

'Dad,' she said, her voice heavy. 'Don't judge this by – by the standards of the past. Mother wouldn't have wanted that. Not ever.'

He took his time replying. 'This is *not* about your mother.'

'Isn't it, though?'

'No, Merc, it's just about basic safe practice. And obviously, there's been at least one fatality. Look, I know accidents happen, but there's no reason to be going out and courting danger. That's the difference here. Your mother, that was an accident. This, this… adventure of Frank's, this was an accident waiting to happen.'

'You've no idea why this was so important to Frank.'

'No, and you've not told me.'

'He didn't want people misinterpreting his actions.'

'Even if it meant ignoring safety restrictions? Come on, Merc.'

The quad-ski slipped and threatened to backslide down the trail's gentle slope. 'Some of these patches are like teflon,' he complained, twitching the drive-stick while he fought to find better purchase.

'It was waxy out by the digsite, too,' she said.

'Digsite? So this is all about what, more of Frank's amateur archaeology? Jeez, Merc, we're paid to refine organics for shipping to the inner system, not to indulge in some futile attempt to uncover the nonexistent biology of a world that's always been dead.'

'See? This is just the attitude Frank was talking about. Closed-minded, jumping to conclusions.'

'Okay, then, I'll open it. You tell me what Frank was up to.'

'He wasn't ready to go pub—'

He's never going to be ready now, he thought. Aloud: 'But it might have some bearing on the rescue. Assuming Joachim's still alive. If I know in advance what the situation is over there.'

Her stance shifted, stiffened somehow, and she fell silent. Slipping into reverie again, he figured. 'You're thinking what?' he asked, quietly.

'Jeez, Dad, nothing. Well, actually, taking a piss.'

Smoother going now. The track was level here, and enviably stable, but he was lost for the next hundred metres in thoughts from the past. Mars, and now Titan. *Once you leave the cradle, the universe will do its best to kill you*, he thought to himself, conscious of how similar – in temperament as well as in appearance – Mercedes was to his memories of her mother.

He spied a relay post, up ahead. He killed the fuel cells, brought the quad-ski to a halt. 'Just going to notify Leto,' he explained, climbing out of the cage. 'Let them know the rescue hasn't been a total failure. Touch wood.' He made his way awkwardly to the bright-blue plastic post that stood like a small totem pole on the cargo track's shoulder, brushed off the crusting, and pressed his communicator against the post's induction pad. Reception was scratchy, but at least there was a link, courtesy of the comm cable. He got through to Rani. She sounded tired, overstressed.

'Mats,' he announced, as though it could be anyone else.

'Oh, thank good— Steen and I were getting worried. Any news?' she asked.

'Some. Not all good. But Merc's alive. Don't know yet about Joachim.'

'Frank?'

'I haven't reached the rover yet, but from what I've heard…'

'Oh.' Pause. 'Let me know the minute you find Joachim. I've had Henna on the link, distraught. As you'd— as you would be.'

'Henna. My God, yes,' he said, realising he'd allowed his own thoughts of personal tragedy to eclipse the larger situation, the uncertainty and grief that Joachim's young wife must now be experiencing. 'How far away from Base is she?'

'Two-three days, still, depending on the storm. She's in the leading hauler. Stopping at every relay post on the route, seems like.'

'Can't blame her.'

'No. Look, Mats, thanks for calling in. Give Merc my love. And bring them back safe.'

'Do my best,' he promised, hoping to sound confident.

Straining to see the track straight ahead of them. The quad-ski's windscreen was positively dark through accumulated gunk. Too bad its own refresh function was on the fritz. They were accordingly going slower than he would have preferred. Twenty-five, was that twenty-five they'd just passed? Ten more to go, then.

'Your mother would have liked Titan,' he commented eventually.

'You think?' Mercedes asked.

'Well, aside from the cold, the dreariness, and the overpressure, and all the toxic gunk. But she'd have liked the geology.'

'Gee, well, when you put it like that…' And he thought, for the first time, he heard a lift in her voice. 'Okay,' she added. 'You want to know what Frank was up to?'

'I want to maximize the chance of getting Joachim back alive… there should never have been three people in that rover, and you know it. Not that I'm not grateful that Joachim was along as a chaperone.' Gruff.

'Big girl now, remember?' Pause. 'Plus, if you must know, *I* was the chaperone.'

'Frank and Joachim? Since when?'

'Couple of years now, I think. It was hardly a secret.'

'I didn't know it.'

'Pretty much everyone else on Base did. You've been pretty closed-off, you know, Dad.'

'Closed off? Since when?'

'Since… since… look, I don't know. Too long.'

'I— wait a minute. Does Henna know this?'

'Yes, Dad, Henna knows. It's *complicated*.'

'It sounds it.'

'Well, like I said, closed off.'

'You were going to tell me what Frank—'

'He's found a platinum-iridium layer.'

'What?'

'That part's actually in the public domain,' she said. 'It's in the Eyre Lacus condensate core, though there's been quite a bit of argument as to whether it's signal or noise. The data's pretty much borderline.'

'But Eyre's a good fifteen hundred klicks away—'

'Two thousand,' she corrected. 'But Frank found a marker, much closer to the topslush, just out in the Mandelbrot lakes region. At that massively eroded site.'

'Doesn't sound like it's worth getting killed over,' Mats said. 'I mean, I assume Frank wasn't checking this out for any reasons of self-sufficiency, or anything actually useful?'

'He had a suspicion,' she replied, and he could hear the iron in her voice, pulling just below the surface. 'He talked to the people he thought would listen openly to what he had to say on the subject, and he didn't bother trying to convert people who wouldn't. I was a tough sell – too much my father's daughter not to be – but what he said stacked up. And what he'd found sounded plausible.'

'So what had he found?'

'He had dates,' she said. 'Well, one date. Sixty-five point five million years.'

Impact. The frisson escaped him, involuntary. 'Sixty-five point five? A platinum-iridium layer, same age as the dinosaur killer? Here on *Titan*?'

'That's the one.'

He thought for a moment. 'No way. That's got to be way off. For one thing, with the rate of precip, you'd have to go a long way down to retrieve samples that old. None of our cores have reached anywhere near that age.'

'Most places that's true,' she countered. 'But the topography around Eyre encourages runoff, that's one of the reasons it was sampled. It's a patchy record, but it does stretch much further back than the other cores. And the radiochem holds up.'

'Okay. Even assuming that's the case, so what? Some large-enough body gets disrupted, too close to Jupiter or whatever, breaks into fragments, part of it hits Earth, kills the dinosaurs, another part slams into Titan. It's all just part of the regular business of solar-system billiards.'

'Yes. But. There's more to it, Dad. He'd run models. *Lots* of them. Any object large enough to do the damage Earth sustained, with a heavy-metal core, would have had to cut so close past Jupiter that the odds against it simultaneously resulting in inner-system and outer-system fragments would be astronomical.'

'No pun intended. But Merc, it only needs to have happened once.'

'But he didn't think it had even happened once. Not through chance. Because in over ten thousand model runs, he never saw any evidence that it could.'

'So what did he say happened? Did he have a theory?'

'Yes, Dad, he had a theory. He thought Earth was just collateral damage. He thought it was *aimed*, and he reckoned the main target was Titan.'

'Did you believe all this?'

'Well, no. And I still don't, I think. Occam's razor. But that's hardly the point.'

Mats thought to respond, thought better of it.

'Thirty-five,' he announced, braking the quad-ski. 'You get some rest?'

'Some, I guess. But I still feel like crap.'

'But you know, if you have some, it'll only make you sick.'

She gave a brief hint of laughter, dead at the birth. 'Don't *joke*, Mats.'

Mats. That pulled him up. One of Pia's expressions, and as near as could be told, her intonation. He rechecked his daughter's med telltales – green, still just a hint of yellow – and blinked away the visions of Martian terrain, a kaleidoscope of eidetic, unwelcomely persistent images. The familiar crinkled salmon-and-sand landscape of the eastern extremity of the Valles Marineris, both before and after the impact. He'd visited Pia out at the encampment, listened patiently while she bubbled over with geologists' anecdotes, tried to discern what it was that captivated her about the surrounding formations. He'd been back a week later to assist with the fruitless rescue attempt, and in case there was anything of Pia to identify. There hadn't been. *Comet core nav cluster malf, impact imminent, VM/Argyre:* the datasquirt had been all the warning anyone on Mars had received, scant seconds before it hit. Out in the field, there likely hadn't been any warning at all. It was still one of the worst catastrophes of the jinxed Martian terraforming effort, but amidst all the public relief that the Hellas Basin communities had been spared, there'd been insultingly little mention of the several dozen lives lost – geologists, tourists, prospectors and miners – in and around Valles Marineris. Mats and his young daughter had left Mars a month later, outbound, as soon as it became obvious that there was no hope of finding any trace of Pia. The campsite had been less than a kilometre from the impact epicentre. But the fanciful notion that Pia might somehow have escaped, might still be lying somewhere in the vast chaos of the Martian southern highlands, tore into him for years afterwards. He'd let her down. He'd left.

'Dad. *Dad!* Brake!' She was reaching for the control stick.

He squinted out the viewscreen, swore, switched the treads to counter-rotation. The quad-ski shuddered, shook, stopped, inched back from the ravine's crumbling edge. 'Sorry,' he mumbled. 'Must've put myself on autopilot.' Checked to ensure they were placed safely out of danger. 'Think we need to do the rest of this on foot.'

'I think you're right,' she said.

*

Just two kilometres; but it took well over an hour before they'd reached the crevasse, the ruined rover. Then there was the necessity to find secure anchorage points for the harpoons they'd brought; to tether the electrically-warmed rope – at Titan temperatures, rope didn't bend, it broke; to secure the rescue harness. Mercedes had pleaded to be the one to climb down, but he'd insisted. Her med telltales were still shading yellow intermittently.

The rover was about eight metres down, turned turtle and angled nose-downslope. Mottled with tholins, snowdrift from the windblown haze.

'She's fallen too far, and the terrain's pretty treacherous, from appearances,' he judged. 'I'd say it's not going to be salvageable.' Which implied, also, that Frank's body, pinned beneath the rover, was beyond retrieval.

Mats's rope skills were rusty, to say the least. That wasn't going to make opening the airlock any easier. He ran over various strategies for gaining entry, as he went hand-over-hand down the rope. But the airlock was open.

Joachim was sprawled awkwardly across the rover's ceiling. His face was caught in a bared-teeth sneer, his unblinking gaze angled down towards the corner to which his helmet had rolled. His skin, though pale, was coloured naturally; it hadn't had time yet to stain, to take on Titan's unwholesome tints. A thin now-frozen trail of something briefly liquid – vomit? bile? – led down from his nostril and the corner of his mouth. Mats felt something gag in his throat – *this is neither the time nor the place for a solid cough, he told himself* – and picked up and reattached Joachim's helmet. Then set about fastening Joachim's body into the rescue harness. He tried not to think too closely about what he was doing.

The rover's cabin had been fairly well sheltered from the force of the shitstorm, but even so. The lack of discoloration on Joachim's skin, in these conditions, sent a clear message as to how recently he'd made his decision.

No need for Mercedes to see that.

'Life support failure,' he told her through the radio. Listened to her breathing break up. Wanted to hold her, to say something that would help. Instead, he toggled the rescue harness's autowinch, pushed the body out through the airlock, watched as the rope took up the strain. In a grim mimicry of life, the harness jerked its slow way upward along the rope.

'There should be a cluster of storage beads in the data-locker,' Mercedes told him, her voice thick and brittle. 'Frank wouldn't want them left behind.'

'OK, got them,' he said, stowing them in his suit's utility pouch. 'Merc, I think we're done here.'

She didn't answer all the time they were carrying Joachim back to the quad-ski. Around them, as the long Titanian afternoon wore on, the sky grew yet darker, more virulent.

They were back in the quad-ski, on the cargo trail in fact, before either of them spoke again.

'Frank say anything about why he thought his impact was aimed? Or by what?'

'He wasn't sure. I mean, sixty-five million years is a pretty long gulf to try to bridge, and I think he was wary of sounding foolish.'

'Even when preaching to the converted?'

'I didn't exactly swallow his ideas hook-line-sinker, just a little more prepared to listen to them. But I think he thought it was all about blinkered viewpoints, competition, stuff like that. Von Neumann machines, maybe. Programmed by life which had arisen elsewhere, under conditions like Titan's. I think his idea was, maybe earth-life, water-based biology, is a bit of a galactic fluke. If the rest of the Galaxy's lifeforms are more like what you'd expect could come out of Titan, like what Frank thought must've arisen on Titan – something purely hydrocarbon-based, or hydrocarbons and nitrogen compounds – then they could see other similar biospheres as a threat, taking the long view, whereas Earth would be Mostly Harmless, so to speak. Even with all its carnosaurs and the like. Not worth a really serious effort to sterilise.'

'That's a fairly long bow to draw,' Mats replied. 'On not a lot of evidence, from the sound of it.'

'Frank knew that, Dad. He knew his ideas were outliers, I think he was fully prepared for them to be shot down, but thought they were important enough to put out there in the first place. Except I think the only person he really communicated them to, the only person he truly trusted with all of it, was Joachim.'

'Huh. That's—'

'Yeah. Dad.'

'What?'

'I wanted to say. What really hurts, really sticks in my craw, is that it's all so random.'

Valles Marineris. 'You're right,' he said. He thought about enlarging on that, decided against it. Gave, instead, space for her – for both of them, really – to be alone with those thoughts. 'Henna will be distraught,' he said finally. Beside him, she nodded. They sat in silence awhile more.

'We will get back there,' she announced. It wasn't a question. 'Someday. Soon, when the weather's cleared. Properly equipped, not just with what the base can spare at the time. So we can check properly on Frank's hypothesis. Hopefully retrieve the rover, too.'

'If you need to do it... exorcizing those demons, or whatever you want to call it...'

'I know. Big girl now. It's not a question of *need*, Dad. It doesn't even matter if Frank was right or wrong, and I know you don't believe he was right. I don't really believe it myself. It's just the right thing to do. For a friend.'

'The whole base is going to be in shock,' Mats said. 'Two out of twelve, gone like that.' He strove to build a mental picture of the two men they'd lost. Realised he'd done the pair of them a disservice, by failing to truly notice them on a day-to-day-basis. What was it Merc had said? Closed-off? Maybe so.

He pondered on the brutality of death in an environment more alien than anything his ancestors could ever have imagined. Reflected on decisions that might have been made. Catalogued his regrets, his losses.

Gave thanks that, eighteen years ago, he'd had the temerity to suggest that a Martian geological expedition's camp was no place for a four-year-old daughter to be staying.

There. That was something to keep hold of.

It wasn't all bad, the past.

hatchway

'Touch me again, and you'll need a proctologist.'

Kalpana's quiet menace is sufficient to persuade Marisol and Django to back away towards the clean white sides of the Hanel West 2 airlock; Stieg, stationed by the lock's inner hatch, sneers 'as if' in response. Only Boris, holding the small tub of baby-blue gel, has the decency to colour up.

'Look, K,' says Django, 'the gel's every bit as vital as the mask, the boots, the gloves. You're, huh, going to get *cold* out there—'

'You think I haven't worked that?' Kalpana replies, her fragile calm slipping, shattering. 'They musta got your plumbing wrong, the shit that comes out sometimes.' As soon as the words are out, she realises they've taken her too far, like they've a tendency to. Too far in, or too far away. Too late now. But she's feeling like a piece of readymeat, underdressed, self-conscious of her plumpness and of the all-important two-three years the group has on her. Of the need to prove she's not just a kid, to do something the dults wouldn't ever dare.

And to show she's worthy. Because *that's* what she's here for, after all. (It's like Boris had said, the first time he'd let slip about the initiation, the test: 'It's all about showing Titan who's boss.')

'I don't think she wants this,' Stieg drawls, leaning for effect against the polished crud-resistant frame that lintels the airlock's inner hatch. Stieg's skinny, a little short, and with skin pale enough that it makes his spiked hair seem blacker than it is. He fixes his eyes on her, then sweeps across

23

the rest of the group. He's playing for an audience. If Boris is the leader, Django the expert, and Marisol the conscience (or perhaps, Kalpana muses, the mascot), then Stieg is the enforcer. Or fancies himself thus, at least. 'You think she wants this? Any of you think she *deserves* this?'

Bastard. There's no way she's going to plead, not in front of a creep like Stieg. But she needs to do *some*thing, to convince them she's not motivated just by fear. She stares past him, feigning boredom with his jibes, affecting a sudden casual interest in the hyperextended saguaro that, foyered inward of the airlock, stands improbably green within its deep bed of grey-orange sand. (Not frozen-hydrocarbon sand, either, but real asteroid-origin *faux*-Earth silica sand. A statement of comparison, or solidarity, or something.)

'It's not *just* about the cold,' Django says, and she's grateful enough for the interjection, for the imperturbability of Boris's younger brother, particularly after her slur. Django handcombs his scruffy crest of orange-brown hair: camo hair, she'd thought it, when first she saw it. 'It's the overpressure. Titan's going to be trying to, huh, push its way in, any way it can. The breathmask covers your face – eyes, ears, mouth, nose. But there's—'

'Grossleaks. Okay, you don't have to paint the picture.' She rubs at her bare forearm, goosefleshed. Unlike the rest of the building, the airlock's not designed for warmth; that's what T-suits are for. None of the group is T-suited. But she's the only one in just a single layer, or in shortsleeves. 'Makes sense. But then, why the ti – uh, the nubs?'

'Sensitivity,' says Boris. 'Ask Marsy.' He makes sufficient of a hand gesture, splaying across his chest, that the tub in his other hand sloshes. Calling it 'gel' is a misnomer, Kalpana decides – some of the *drinks* she's experimented with have been gluggier.

Marisol, for her part, turns awkwardly away. Maybe she's not willing to be used as an example, or maybe she's still pissed with Boris, from last week.

'It's too runny,' says Kalpana, trying not to whine. 'It's just going to run straight off—'

'*Told* you she doesn't want this,' says Stieg, staring her down.

'Shut *up*, tool,' Boris says, glaring at Stieg. The latter shrugs, indifferent to the other's height and bulk.

'So you need to add it last,' Django explains. 'That's one of the reasons for the loose shirt and shorts – it makes it easier to, huh, slap on the goop quickly. As well as for movement once you get outside. But it *has* to be runny at three hundred K, if it's to have any elasticity at one hundred.'

'We can delay this if you'd rather,' suggests Marisol – and something's up, something's bugging her, because Marisol is not looking at Kalpana's face, not at all, while she speaks. It's as if instead she's conversing with Boris's tub of gel. 'We don't have to do this today.' There's almost a plea in her voice, Kalpana reckons.

And Kalpana would readily enough defer. Now that she's arrived at the moment, it's as though there's a premonition, a foretaste of the overpressure. It's strong enough, this feeling, to cause her breath to catch, to send her heart on such a rush of activity beneath her breast that it's sure to catch the boys' attention. She's not even sure, right at this instant, that this is a group she wants to be accepted by: up close, they've lost some of the initial rebellious gloss, the dult-defying omnipotence that she'd first glimpsed, or thought she'd glimpsed. Up close, there's more than a hint of the dult in how they're treating her, right now. But there's Stieg: and she *will not* give Stieg the slightest hint of satisfaction. This is the bravest, stupidest, most illegal thing she's ever attempted, and she will not give him reason to taunt her.

Hanel West 2 airlock is cold. It smells of burnt bleach, baked dust, and cryogrease, and it's cold.

'No,' says Kalpana, trying, and signally failing, to catch Marisol's eye. 'No, we don't have to. But today makes sense, with all the dults either at the loftball game, or the concert.'

'She's right,' agrees Boris, as though this settles it. And maybe it does.

'Right. Then I'm ready. Five-three-one-four-six, right?'

'Five-three-*four-one*-six,' Django corrects her.

Whoops.

*

25

She'd been seven, almost eight, when it happened. When her mother pushed her father through the hatchway.

Kalpana had mental images from that day. They'd never leave her. She'd made, from the images, a loosely-arranged sequence; but it was a knotted thing, and as difficult to follow as it was painful. It wasn't until a full year later that her aunt had been able to assemble for Kalpana a narrative, a sufficiently-detailed framework through which to comprehend the day's events.

To comprehend; but not to understand.

They'd been living in Clemence, a small single-arcology community of never more than a hundred souls, on the southern edge of the Senkyo dunefields. It wasn't Kalpana's first home, nor even the third – miners were itinerant, almost by definition, and the Brauns certainly fitted that pattern – but it was the earliest place of which she retained solid memories.

Ultimately, all of those memories led back to the airlock.

She wasn't sure how long the pharmhands had been living in the community: several months, certainly, maybe even a year. But families in Clemence came and went all the time, as processing and extraction fluctuated at the various mining operations among the coffee-dark dunes to the north and the sepia-stained knobbled highlands to the south and east. Among adults, friendships weren't sought out overmuch, because why bother establishing ties with a group of people who might well have moved on within twelve months? Among children of Kalpana's age, friendships were understood to be temporary, and subject to mysterious external influence – a best friend might be taken, with but few days' notice, to a mining community several hundred klicks away. You tended, after awhile, to learn not to elevate anyone to 'bestfriend' status, but merely to maintain a circle of near-equidistant acquaintances. (Or you could communicate by feed, with friends who really meant something, but Kalpana had never found that satisfying – what was the point of talking to someone if you weren't actually in the same place?)

So the pharmhands had been in the arcology for months, posing as miners. Until they were outed, by someone. She'd assumed, after the fact, that it must have been her father who'd notified the pol, but Kalpana's aunt thought it more likely he'd just been scapegoated. 'Made an example of,' she'd explained. 'Over some pack of sick fucks' desire – pardon my Esperanto, *but* – to maximise their profit. And to keep the punters intimidated.'

It had unfolded slowly to start with.

The pharmhands gave no show of awareness that the pol would be at the arcology within a few hours (though they must have known, if everyone else did). But the pharmhands had weapons, and they gathered up all of Clemence's population and assembled them in the foyer in front of one of the arcology's inner airlocks. The sparse crowd of perhaps sixty people – miners, merchants, retirees, children – were made to stand in front of the foyer's synth-stone fountain showpiece. The constant splashing of water across the scales of the fountain's giant sculpted carp was a distraction: Kalpana hoped they wouldn't be kept standing here for too long.

Two of the pharmhand women sported thick red goggles and held HD mining lasers, very probably the same lasers that had been used to blind and incapacitate Clemence's own modest security cadre. The laserwielders stood and stared threateningly at anyone in the crowd (including, from time to time, Kalpana herself) who might look to move too close, or to escape. Another woman held up a small shiny phial, which might contain phloo, or perhaps something worse. Three pharmhand men, also goggled, searched the crowd for someone, and stopped in front of Horst and Rashmi Braun, Kalpana's parents, whom they took out the front of the group. Kalpana moved to accompany them, but was booted forcefully back by one of the laser-carriers.

She was scared, and winded, and humiliated at the kick, and puzzled at what the pharmhands could want with her parents – were they to be given the psychoactive virus? Her gaze twisted to the woman who held the phial aloft, but the woman's pose did not shift.

On the other side of the armed guards, two of the men manoeuvred Kalpana's father into place, his back to the crowd, in the corridor just in front of the inner airlock hatch. A third held her mother, who struggled in the rough embrace until a phrase muttered in her ear persuaded her to relent, while another man – Mikhail Tulleyrand – permaglued her father's elbows, at shoulder height, to either side of the hatch frameway. This, in Kalpana's eyes, underscored both the pharmhands' cruelty and their obtuseness. She now guessed that their intention was to make her father stand, for hours or days, as punishment. She'd read about this sort of thing in her history sims just a few days ago, the petty barbarism of war, mistreatment of prisoners. Her fear subsided somewhat. The Pol would be here in much less than a day, and then the pharmhands would be caught, her parents freed. And although it would probably hurt immensely, her father wouldn't necessarily need to be unglued: he could just get these arms, these 'C-fibre-cored full-sensation prosthetics', replaced, same as he'd had to replace his *proper* arms after the accident at the Mezzoramia brinemine, when his T-suit had been pinned in an iceslip.

The pharmhands were evil and stupid men and women who deserved to be captured. They didn't recognise that her father had artificial arms, and they clearly didn't understand that the pol would be at the arcology within a few short hours.

Then they permaglued Horst Braun's hands to the sides of his balding head, just above the ears, and it began to be more problematic.

She's pulling on the mask, a standard home-closet emergency rig of some thick clear plastic, rimmed with a flabby polymer seal, wishing they'd all give her a bit more space. She's not claustrophobic, of course, but she's nonetheless feeling crowded, set-upon. And the mask has a whiff of that tholin stink to it, somewhere between nicotine and putrefaction, which certainly doesn't help.

If she's going to do this, she'd rather just get on. But Kalpana knows that any under-prep, any mistake, could be fatal. Belatedly, she wonders if she's fit enough. It'd be ironic, or worse than, if she were to break a limb or something, after all her aunt's daily exercise reminders, her weekly '*Titan may be slow, but it's not soft*' cautions, her monthly osteo horror stories.

(As if Kalpana, of all people, needs any more of *those*. After what happened to her father.)

Then Boris taps her on the shoulder, almost apologetic. 'You'll need this,' he explains, and hands her a shaped papery filter, evidently designed to fit across nose and mouth.

'Why?' she asks. 'Isn't the mask gas-tight?'

'It's not for gas,' begins Marisol, who's still not looking directly at Kalpana. In the dry blue light of the airlock, Marisol's face, framed in a synth-fur hoodover, looks as cold as Kalpana's feels. The Hanel West 2 airlock is freezing. But, of course, as cold goes...

'Plus you can't expect the seal to be as effective at one hundred K – it'll be more brittle, inflexible. Along with everything else,' says Django. 'Atmosphere isn't an issue, huh, long as you don't blow a total leak. You won't be out long enough. But the tholin's a killer, if you breathe it in.'

'Bad enough on your *skin*,' says Boris.

'Getting scared now?' Stieg taunts.

'*Lid* it, tool,' Boris replies.

'Scared? No,' she says, too loud. She undoes the mask, slips the filter in place, suffers Marisol to refasten the mask with spindly fingers.

Boris is still holding the tub of goop. Expectantly. Like Kalpana's a wankbot or something. She meets his stare, waits for him to turn aside. But though he colours up again, to the point that his cheeks approximate the russet of his moptop, Boris is *in charge*, and doesn't concede authority readily. (Obviously. Else Stieg would be running things.)

'I'm not putting that on while you lot are in the room,' she announces, eventually. 'Can't you just come back for it, once I'm out of the airlock?'

'It's worth credits,' says Django. 'Not cheap.'

'So?'

'So, you leave it in the airlock, it gets contammed. No,' says Boris.

Kalpana rolls her eyes. 'Right. But you can still shut me in here. No way I'm putting it on with you lot gawping.'

'As if you've got anything we haven't seen better elsewhere,' says Stieg, attracting a glare from Marisol.

'I *mean* it,' Kalpana continues. 'I can knock on the hatch when I'm done, before I step out. Best deal you're going to get.'

Boris weighs it. 'Make sure you do round the mask,' he says, handing her the tub. 'As well.' He motions the others towards the inner hatch.

Alone at last, she's newly conscious of the loudness of her breathing, the sticky sweat at her armpits, the airlock's oppressive silent chill. The weight of the tank against her back. Her heart's racing, and something – besides just the mask's rebreather – feels stuck in her mouth. She moves to the inner wall, to the corner she judges best to be out of sight from the hatch's viewscreen, and does the daubing. Squatting down for the private bits.

'Don't thump so loud,' Boris complains, stepping back into the lock when she's finished. 'You want the dults to hear?'

She holds the tub of gel out to him. 'All plugged,' she says, smirking.

He takes the tub from her gloved hand, throws a distasteful glance at his now-sticky fingers.

'See you on the other side,' she says, distinctly more upbeat than she feels. 'Five-three-four-one-six, right?'

'Uh… yeah. Right.' He's coloured up again, whatever *that's* about. He gives her a look she can't interpret, and closes the hatch behind him.

Right. She swallows, presses the sequence of commands. If Django's correct – and she's not sure what she hopes, right now – this is the only airlock in Hanel she can leave from, the only one that'll open out for a non-T-suited occupant.

There's perhaps five seconds during which nothing happens. Then there's a thrum, from somewhere beneath the ridged C-plate decking, and the airlock floods with a gush of cylinder-cold nitrogen, chill as frozen cotton against every stretch of exposed skin. The mask's seal presses in, instantly, all around the perimeter of her face, and she opens her mouth in startled reaction. The faceplate fogs with escaped moisture.

She hadn't, she realises, been freezing before this. Now she can't stop shivering. The gel sticking the seam of her shorts to herself is starting to feel unpleasantly spiky as it chills. She braces her bared arms against her chest, then peels them awkwardly away. The airlock's blue lights fade until all within is navy and black, save for a rim of dim light around the outer hatchway. The way out.

Two minutes, she tells herself. *Just two minutes. Might as well get it over with.*

She pushes on the outer hatch. There's some resistance, but the pressure differential is now slight enough that the exertion is mild. The outer hatch opens, onto Titan's drear twilight.

The airlock, it turns out, has in fact been warm. To human skin, Titan is colder than space itself. She'd swear her neck, her arms, her legs were clad in ice-chilled armour.

She steps out. Into a landscape cold enough, given time, to liquefy the oxygen in her lungs.

The pharmhands didn't hurry. They'd now glued her father's boots to the corridor decking, the toes of his boots a handspan behind the hatchway opening. One of the pharmhands still held him up, though she didn't see why they needed to. He'd stopped struggling, and he was fastened by feet and elbows.

Kalpana was worried – it was scary to see your mother and father so upset, and not to know exactly why all of this was happening – but she was fairly sure that whatever the pharmhands were trying, it wasn't going to work. The pol would be here long before her father got too tired to stand, and they'd get him free, and capture the criminals. And even if the pharmhands were thinking of something worse, like shooting him – and they had weapons beyond just the lasers, the first guns Kalpana had ever seen, in real life – why would they have glued her father in the frame like that?

Or they might've been planning to open the outer lock – which would kill everybody, including the pharmhands because none of them were wearing T-suits – but she didn't think even pharmhands were stupid enough to do that. And they might be using her father as a lock-shield, to stop the pol entering through this airlock, but there were three other entrances into Clemence, and the pharmhands weren't moving to block those ones off. They were standing around, in this one, waiting.

Waiting for what?

The man with the glue-tube, Tulleyrand, tossed it to a subordinate, and turned to face the crowd held captive by the threat of laser-fire.

'You can save him,' he said, his voice loud, brassy, and surprisingly polite. His hair looked too dark for his skin, and he wasn't tall like Kalpana's father, nor broad, but he held himself exactly like someone big enough to beat up anyone he liked. He gestured with the palm of his hand. 'Just tell us who squirted the pol, and we'll cut Braun free.'

There was some shuffling within the crowd, but it amounted to nothing.

'I'm not a patient man,' the pharmhand's leader warned. 'Two minutes. Then it happens.'

What happens? Kalpana wondered. She genuinely was frightened by now, with the deadline's precision, the still-mysterious threat. Because this man didn't sound stupid, like he should do. He sounded *dangerous*.

Her mother, still herself pinioned, turned to look over the crowd, as though she was hoping to see someone, or something. Kalpana waved, but her mother, shaking, face striped with damp, did not acknowledge the gesture.

Whatever her mother was looking for, she didn't see it. Then, turning back to face the tableau that was her husband, she said something.

'Beg pardon?' Tulleyrand asked, leaning as if to hear.

'I said *I did it*,' announced her mother, voice roughened in a way Kalpana had never before heard.

'You?'

'Yes. Now let him down.' She coughed. Swallowed. '*Please.*'

'No. No, I don't think so, Ms Braun,' replied Tulleyrand, addressing the crowd. 'Though high marks for the delaying tactic, I think. *One* minute.' And he leaned forward again, exaggerated, theatrical, and whispered something to her.

Whatever he'd said – and Kalpana wasn't close enough to hear – it caused Rashmi Braun to struggle against her confines, with sufficient violence that her captor (who outmassed her by at least her own bodyweight) had considerable difficulty in retaining his footing. Another pharmhand moved to assist; the women with the lasers tightened their grips, and made mock-strafing gestures across the face of the crowd; Tulleyrand, his face a study in amusement, announced 'We won't keep you,' and started counting down the seconds from thirty.

When he got to five, it all went to shit.

The skin burns. It is so cold that each movement she makes – and it's now move, or die – is accompanied by a pain so sharp, so solid, that the body suspects it to be heat, for 'cold' could never be this extreme.

She is out on Titan.

She is out on Titan, *sans* T-suit. Directly in front of her is a man-made anomaly, a statement of solidified irony, an object misplaced upon this wide brown land. A saguaro cactus, carved from water-ice, stands guard upon the apron of cleared ground that leads away from the airlock. Erstwhile twin to the still-growing cactus within the arcology's foyer, the ice cactus has been turned, in the two years since its erection, to a translucent tea-brown by windblown tholins and sand grains. It is stained most deeply upon its western flanks.

Behind the ice saguaro, the sky is choked by a vague, impenetrable ceiling of fuscous haze. The ground slopes gently down, bouldered in a palette that spans from tangerine, through the darkest possible orange, through brown, to black. To her north, beyond the ochre-smeared, muck-raddled apron in which the cactus is embedded, the horizon is flanked by the haze-murked umber ridge of the nearest of Belet's long parallel dunes. Leading past the cactus – towards the near-endless foothills that are the dunefields – the paths made by boot, ski, or tread are indistinct, only marginally less cluttered by ice pebbles and clumped sand drifts than the rest of the intervening terrain.

She takes in the late-afternoon view within a couple of instants, conscious that time is short. Hanel West Cargo 4 is five paces to the right of the Hanel West 2 airlock outer hatch, ninety degree right turn, twenty paces further. She's walked it dozens of times, in the sims, she's got it

down to sixteen seconds. But the sims aren't rigged for skin-sense. And with the goop solidifying at her seams, the rubbed-raw chill scraping at the skin of her arms, legs, and neck, the frozen-cotton armour of shirt and shorts, the walk to the corner is many more than just five paces.

Breathe through your mouth, she urges. Yet even that is difficult.

If she slips, falls, she is almost assuredly dead, since she will be instantly cold-welded to the orange-brown icy skin of Titan. (And at this, a phrase of her father's comes back, one of the few she can genuinely remember, though she's not sure it's his true voice: 'You make a mistake on Titan, you'll be instantly dead. Even if you're not dead instantly.') Thick air, lazy grav, surfaces that cannot be trusted: it's *measured, or dead*. So she plants each boot with sleepwalk-slow caution, checks the rightness of the step before shifting weight forward to the front foot, while flakes of breeze-borne tholin adhere, malevolent brown-black snow, against her bare arms.

The first few flakes melt; but after this, they do not. They stick, solid on solid.

Her limbs are duller. The atmosphere seems to grow ever thicker (though this must be illusion), the ground so close to the arcology wall is treacherously slick in patches, with the memory of waste-heat leakage. The mask presses against her face, pinches against her cranium. Each breath of tanked air comes cold, rasping, rattling its way to her lungs, which ache with indrawn chill. Her joints complain, and every crusted glob of goop pinches, scrapes, snags with each protesting movement. The shorts sure don't help, merely provide a strip of frigid inter-thigh sandpaper; she wonders why none of them has instead suggested a skirt. Marisol, you would have thought, at least... But *nothing* about this is as it was in the sims, not even the visuals.

A horrible thought occurs: she has only the others' word that they've already managed this, that they've proved it possible to survive this. She might, in truth, be first, a guinea-pig.

But why would they lie?

She rounds the corner, not wanting to think of how long it has taken. Each step a risk, each second's exposure an increment of damage.

35

If her skin freezes too much, it will crack at the joins, and then the first flake of tholin to reach her freezing bloodstream will likely kill... eventually. There's no place that does carcinogens quite like Titan.

Five-three-four-one-six. It *was* 'four-one', wasn't it?

Django had reckoned two minutes would be safe, probably. But at this shuffle, two minutes, or whatever fraction of that remains since she left the 'lock, may not get her to the cargo entryway.

And she slips. Her left foot skids back, her right knee bends painfully, and she falls forward, in sudden languid dread. She stretches her arms out in front, braces against the jolt that hits when her gloves press into the icy brown gravel. Her knees – left back, right forward – both come within centimetres of the chilled flypaper that, to bared human skin, is Titan's surface. Heart rattling within its freezing cage, she stands and cannot stop from shaking at the nearness of the death from which she has just escaped. She has either bitten her tongue, or caught it, somehow, on the rebreather. She is too intimidated to take another step, yet she must. So she does. Her ankle lances with a pain straight and sharp enough to thread needles.

And then she hears the voice.

It was a bump, a push. It could well have been accidental, though as time passes, Kalpana becomes more convinced that it was a deliberate shove, an execution. One of the pharmhands, struggling to help keep Kalpana's mother Rashmi contained, knocked into the neighbouring guard's back, with the result that Rashmi, with a despairing and disbelieving cry, was propelled forward against her husband. Horst Braun was thus pushed forward through the open inner hatch of the airlock. The shaped C-fibre rods that comprised the 'bones' within Braun's prosthetic arms butted against, and pivoted around, the unyielding rim of the hatchway frame; the C-fibre-boned hands of his prostheses were pushed inwards. The right side of his skull caved in with a sickening wet crack, audible over (and cutting short) his shocked scream. And Kalpana's father, still glued by the elbows, hung limp as a rag doll, blood running from the broken-eggshell mess of the side of his head, beneath his still-glued hand.

The crowd's forward surge was arrested as the guards flashed off a sequence of blue-white warning shots which left almost everyone temporarily blinded by the reflections from the fountain. There followed a disorganised press of bodies, the chaotic disquiet punctuated by a couple of loud, sharp noises, and when Kalpana's sight returned, Mikhail Tulleyrand lay dead, his head apparently rammed hard against the hatch's unforgiving frame. Near Tulleyrand's feet, Kalpana's mother too was dead, from a single clean gunshot wound to her chest.

There was the smell of shit in the air, and vomit, and something else.

The half-dozen surviving pharmhands fled, in several vehicles, to one or more of the neighbouring small mining settlements.

The pol arrived by plane from Sagan four hours later, and having established that Kalpana had no surviving kin within the arcology, took her back with them: she had an aunt and, she thought, a cousin in Sagan. She'd met them once, or perhaps twice.

The days that followed were hollow and long.

Two of the pharmhands, a contracted couple, were eventually caught. But the population of the small mining communities was itinerant by nature, and it was easy to pass unnoticed provided you had the skills to pretend to be someone you were not.

It was easy, too, provided one was patient, and discreet, to find a few buyers for your lucrative stockpile of psychoactive viruses. The pharmhands would not have existed without demand for their products.

'What do you mean, the wrong numbers?' Django's voice, or Boris's. She's not sure which.

'Django?' she calls, in response.

'I mean they've changed them since yesterday, huh, I've no idea why.' *This* one's Django. Which means the other was Boris.

'Django?' she repeats. 'Guys? Anybody?'

A woman's voice, Marisol's, cuts in across her. It's obvious they haven't heard Kalpana. 'So she can't get back in through Cargo 4? What about backtracking to H West 2?'

Django answers. 'It's only a minute into purge. I don't see how it'd let us open it for another fifteen minutes or so, huh. She'll be cryopork by then.'

'I don't *believe* this! We can't just let this all turn to shit – can we get *today's* numbers for her?'

'It'll take time,' replies Django. The sound in her earbud is tinny, ineffectual, she needs to hold still to hear it. Except that holding still is exactly what she *doesn't* need to do. Every part of her stings, now, with cold and maybe also with abrasion.

She has scarcely rounded the corner.

The makeshift path that leads along the arcology wall, to Hanel West Cargo 4 entryway still fifteen impossible metres distant, is slick and somehow waxy. In front of the cargo entryway, the clutch of randomly-parked vehicles – a couple of quad-skis, a rover, and a few ancient and mistreated skid-bikes – stand like a murk-enshrouded, misplaced flotilla, their indifference to the environment a private insult. *We* belong out here, they seem to say. But *you*—

The terrain itself is not so ready with rejection: the dun wasteland all around is waiting to embrace her, to never let her go. She's finding it difficult to remember why she's been resisting.

It's all about showing Titan who's boss.

No group, no gang, however enticing, could possibly be worth this. She's been a fool to think otherwise.

The earbud buzzes back into activity. 'It'll take too long,' Django repeats. 'And we couldn't get the numbers to her, anyhow. Her rig's on transmit-only, huh, it's not set up for reception.'

Idiots. Total fucking incompetents. She unleashes a compact string of further obscenities, confident they'll never reach their target.

She manages another step, does her best to ignore the pain scything along her legs. The tank on her back, her precious air supply, feels to be growing progressively heavier with each passing second. The visor is now so fogged that she must guess, and work from memory, to interpret the dimming, fuzz-enveloped shapes that are the arcology wall, the stand of work vehicles, the terrain in front of her. Her hands have become an encumbrance, a-tingle within the thoroughly inadequate protection of the gloves, her arms at once so numb and so afire with cold agony that she cannot hold them in front of her, and yet she surely needs the protection should she stumble again. Even if it shatters her fingers in the process.

'If it's transmit-only, then how come we haven't heard from her?' Boris's voice asks.

'Who cares?' asks another voice. Stieg's. 'I mean, who fucking *cares*? She wouldn't have—'

'Shut *up!*' says Boris, and even through the earbud's crappy acoustics, she can hear the edge in his voice, the knife of desperation. (It's his head that stands to roll for this, if hers gets frozen through.) 'Honest-to-fuck, tool, what've you got in for her?'

And at that, somehow, she realises. She's been hearing it wrong. It's not 'tool'. Not quite.

Boris doesn't know, obviously. Kalpana never did, from the start. But now she does.

She'd never thought to bother with their surnames. Surnames were a *dult* thing, an irrelevance… until it turns out that they tell you everything you think you need to know.

And Kalpana Braun, gagging in her shock on the rebreather, still has no idea how she's going to fight her way through into the safety of Hanel West Cargo 4; but she knows damn well she's going to find it, somehow. As soon as she's shuffled, half-blind, along the next fifteen metres. Because there's no way on this big orange-brown world that she's going to provide Stieg Tulleyrand with such a convenient cure for his hatred, his emptiness, and his pain.

39

broadwing

They were flying above Hotei, traversing the region that his mother always insisted on calling the Browneye, when Åke realised something was wrong. Not something in the terse and acidic exchanges between his parents – *that* was a constant, bubbling through under the edges of his sim – but something more technical, more fundamental, more acutely dangerous. He emerged from his sim, slipped his tether, and moved forward along the aisle toward the cockpit.

'Should've skirted the rim,' his father was saying, burly frame strapped awkwardly into the co-pilot's alcove. One brawny arm overflowing, resting on a panel of instruments that presumably weren't crucial, or touch-sensitive. 'Least there's a decent few settlements scattered along that way. Airstrips, I mean to say.'

'Oh, for cock's sake!' Åke's mother snapped back. 'Let *me* do the flying, OK, Todd?' His mother was bird-like. Intense. Straight black hair, cropped sharp. She sharpened her words too. None of her syllables dared linger.

His father's voice was languid, rough, like unevenly weathered stone. A little gravelly. 'I'm just saying—'

'I know just what the cock you're saying! You could show some cocking *respect* for my expertise,' said his mother, eyes flicking nervily between the windscreen's view and the bank of instruments below it. 'I don't tell *you* how to do your geochem.'

Respect. That was bad. Åke hastened to find a group of words with which he could deflect, defuse, steer the talk to a safer place.

His father beat him to it. 'Yeah, well you could be a bit less goddamn blasé about—'

Åke coughed, loud enough to be heard over the thrum of the engines, loud enough to distract his mother from her semi-automatic response. 'Is there some kinda problem?' he asked, trying to sound sleepy, shuffling forward into the space between their berths.

'No, Oak, it's all looking fine,' she replied, gesturing towards the windscreen's dreary Titanian vista: brown sky, grainy-looking in the falling light, darker brown horizon. The cockpit's lighting, blue-tinged, seemed cheap and unreal in contrast.

It was unusually dark for this time of month. Åke couldn't remember ever having seen so much cloud cover. 'Is it a storm?' he asked.

'No storm. Just—'

'The boy's no fool, Junko. Why can't you ever be goddamn *straight* with him?'

'Todd, I *am* being straight. Shut the cock *up*.' The edge again. Never there when she addressed Åke himself; always when she spoke at his father. As though there were two of her, superpositioned. A quantum pair.

'Is it going to rain?' Åke persisted.

'No, Oak,' his mother said. 'It's not going to rain. Not on my flight.' She attempted a smile, but it just conveyed as thin and forced.

'How can you *know* that, Junko?' his father asked, brandishing her name like a swear-word. 'You've seen those clouds. And the runway at Porco was *wet*. How the hell can—'

The plane lurched. Not much, but enough to let a flicker of indecision play across his mother's stern, determined face. And enough to unsettle something in the logjam of the aft luggage compartment. It sounded like one of his dad's sample canisters. His father swore, unbuckled himself, squeezed past Åke, heading back.

42

The chorus of engines dipped and strengthened, a faltering hymn to redundant engineering. Ahead, the craggy line of the horizon pushed its way up the windscreen, then receded. It seemed to leave the glass more deeply stained, like a tide-mark. Åke heard his father grumbling over the baggage, and weighed up his prospects for getting to sit for a time in the co-pilot's berth.

Better not, he reckoned.

'If there's no problem,' he asked, slow, loud enough that both parents should hear, 'why does it matter whether we fly across it, or around?'

Nobody answered.

The plane was a Volker Broadwing, a squat, slow, twelve-engined craft, three small tandem pushmi-pullyu electroprops on each wing. It handled, his mother said, like a sleep-deprived hippo, but this, Åke gathered, was almost a compliment: Titan's winds were gentle enough, for the most part, but they could get pushy.

Åke's initial elation at the news their holiday would require flight had not survived the revelation that they'd be taking a rental Broadwing rather than one of her company craft. The reasons she'd given when he'd asked, repeatedly, had involved credit, insurance, liability. Typical grownup stuff.

The Volker might as well have been a bus. Or a monorail cabin. A Xu-33 Lufter, the type of craft his mother regularly piloted, would have had them *home* by now, easy, not still rattling through the airborne muck above north-central Hotei, still an hour or more out from Solà.

They'd been visiting relatives, his father's mostly, in Porco, a ten-home arcology situated on one of the south-eastern foothills skirting Arcus, the crumbling brown ice-rock ridge that wrapped itself around the southern edge of Hotei Regio's ice-filled central basin. The flight northeast – five hours at two hundred klicks per – had held Åke's attention, pretty much: there was something special about seeing your home from this kind of altitude, high enough that the details got smudged by the dirty air.

And as the flight progressed, as Solà's familiar terrain had receded, there'd been the sense of exploration. Discovery, almost. Like a sim, except this was *real*. The landing on groomed ice, at Porco's field – the builders at Porco had had to shave off the top of a hill, to get enough flat expanse for the village's airstrip – had felt thrilling and just that bit dangerous, with the braking skids not really starting to grip for the first several hundred metres of touchdown. His mother had joked about nearly having to use the grapnels, but she'd brought it to a stop in good order.

The holiday itself, though, the visit... *that* had been hell. Porco was so much smaller than he'd imagined, there was nothing for him to *do* and his cousins all resented him for having grown up somewhere bigger and more interesting than where they themselves lived, as though that was *his* fault. Virtually the only positive experience of the whole vacation had been a local midnight trip outside, T-suit and all, in the company of his uncle Wiremu. His uncle, a frustrated astronomer (on Titan, what other kind?), had climbed with him to the crest of a broad icy ridge, and had pointed out Saturn. Uncle Wiremu had waited until Åke's eyes had acclimatised to the thick, opaque darkness, until he'd made out the faint dark smudge, the ghost of a ghost that marked the immense orb and the rings. Afterwards, walking back in the sudden glare of their T-suits' helmet lamps, carefully retracing their path down the side of the ridge, Åke couldn't fully visualise the shape he'd seen in the darkness, but the fact of it burned within him. He'd seen *Saturn*. From Solà, Saturn was perpetually just below the eastern horizon. Here, it was always slightly up, though generally invisible in the gloomy orange glare of daylight.

But even then, the spell had been broken within minutes of their return. They'd been late for the midday meal, according to the arcology's day-cycle, and Uncle Wiremu hadn't properly explained where they'd be going. The cousins seemed newly suspicious of Åke, as though he'd yet again breached some undeclared code of conduct. They mocked him with renewed enthusiasm.

And his parents squabbled constantly. There was none of the reprieve that would have applied back in Solà: neither of them had work to report to, Porco was too small and too uninteresting to invite repeated exploration by either of them, and Åke couldn't drop in on Aleish, or Kasper, or Zac like he normally would have in such circumstances. (Nor could he find the privacy to do his sim, beyond just fleetingly.) Finally, even the weather conspired, with methane rain, or at least its threat. He was confined to the same too-small cluster of rooms with his parents. They couldn't agree on plans for the day, on memories of prior commitments, on the need to keep up appearances. Nor on a thousand things besides. Bickering. Sledging. Undermining. Two weeks, a Titan month. It had, exactly, been hell.

'Think you guys need to suit up,' his mother announced, as matter-of-fact as though she was issuing a teeth-brushing reminder.

'So there's a problem, all of a sudden?' The words were an offhand grenade, lofted by Åke's father, now coming forward from the freight alcove.

'Shut the cock *up*, Todd,' she replied, focusing her attention between the controls and the windscreen. Her knuckles were white, and she was leaning forward as though that would somehow offer her clearer vision through the murk. '*You* want to fly the cocking thing?'

'No, you're doing fine,' he said. All the fight seemed suddenly to leave him; just a weariness remained. 'How bad is it?'

'Piece of cocking *string*,' she said. 'How the cock should *I* know? I don't even know what's causing the problem, and the plane itself reckons there *isn't* a problem. But the power transmission to the engines is erratic, and trending worse.'

'How much worse?'

'Are we going to crash?' Åke asked, his voice fluting. His insides went numb, in an unfamiliar and thoroughly intimidating manner.

'Cock, Todd! Like I said, you need to suit *up*.' Her voice found time, amongst everything, to soften slightly. 'You too, Oak.'

'Mum, are we going to crash?' Åke repeated, while his father, fully serious now, went aft to fetch the T-suits.

'No, Oak, honey,' she replied. 'We're not going to crash. We're just going to land much too suddenly. And hard.' The plane shifted a bit, more yaw than pitch, as if for emphasis.

'But—'

'Not *now*, Oak. Suit time.'

There'd barely been time for him to suit up. And though he had indeed managed to occupy the co-pilot's berth for the landing (while his father tethered and braced himself against the passenger compartment's forward bulkhead), the experience hadn't been at all as he'd hoped. The berth's seat, now in crash-couch mode, was designed for an adult and wouldn't properly conform to Åke's suited figure.

The landing was rough. His mother had spied an approximately flat stretch of ground, the delta of some eroded, morained, long-obsolete drainage channel, in the last minute or so that she'd been able to keep the Volker airborne. (It was plainly no landing-strip, was littered with pebbles of ice or rock, but a touchdown in the surrounding tholin-stained hillocks and gullies would have been catastrophic.) Through the windscreen the landscape loomed, growing slowly larger and taking on smudgy details until it was so impossibly close that Åke became convinced that they must somehow have touched down already; then they struck, with unnerving violence.

It was lumpier than it had looked.

The impact sheared off at least one, maybe two of the skids, at the first moment of contact. From there it was an uncontrolled, bruising shake-and-slide across the rubble-field, with the listing left wing threatening to gyre them every time it scraped into the uneven icy surface beneath it. The final skid snapped, audibly distinct from the scratchy clatter of the slide and the thud of outcrops against the Volker's hardened-polymer underside, and then the plane abraded itself to an awkward, disturbing stop. A brutal silence, punctuated only by the amplified gush of his own breathing. His mouth sharp with the tang of reflux, his gloved palms impotently slick with sweat, Åke willed his heart to calm. He'd bitten his cheek in panic.

They were down.

His father, fully suited like Åke, grunted. His mother had refused to put on her own suit before the landing; not that there'd been the opportunity, in any case. She read the controls, unstrapped herself, and pulled herself upright, rubbing her forearm. Her T-suit beckoned plaintively from the floor near her feet.

'We're intact,' she announced, as though they were collectively some kind of precious porcelain heirloom: The Family Garrity, in bone china. 'Radio's dead, which is a cocking *bitch*, but life support, climate control, and everything else seems solid. Except—'

'Yes?'

'Shit. Cock.' Her eyes flicked from point to point within the plane's interior, like a wary sparrow seeking sanctuary. 'Shit!' She bent, now, to pick up her suit and helmet.

'*What?*' his father asked, his growl made tinny by the suit's acoustics.

'That smell. You can't – ? No, of course.' Her nostrils flared. 'We have a leak.'

She began pulling on the T-suit, climbing into it as though into the world's most cumbersome pair of overalls. Åke couldn't believe how calm she was, which was terrifying in itself. Legs; then the gloves and sleeves of the arms, and the chest; and then collapsing down the sectors of the neck-ring so that it formed a single thick flange; then the helmet. All of it without evident hurry, or any trace of panic; and yet every second, more of Titan was apparently seeping its deadly way into the cabin, and therefore her lungs. His heart thundering out of control, Åke held his breath in futile, vicarious solidarity, and it was only when she'd sealed the helmet (and exhaled loudly into the suit's mic) that he realised she'd been holding her own breath for most of the last two minutes.

'Are you—' his father began, bending towards her.

'Todd, I'm *fine*,' she snapped back, and then coughed so ominously that Åke moved to steady her against a fall. 'A little dust,' she added weakly, before coughing again with more semblance of control. She spat expertly into the helmet's narrow internal sluice. 'We need to find the leak.'

'Probably easier to spot from outside,' his father suggested, moving towards the airlock.

'Todd, wait, we need to—'

The plane, unbalanced by the motion within, shifted slightly on some fulcrum under their feet, and then settled. The floor now sloped the other way.

'Todd, we have to kill the electrics.' She turned to check something on the Broadwing's control panel.

'What? Are you cra—'

'No, the *leak*. Unless we can stop the leak, the atmosphere's going to shift ever closer to a flammable mix. Probably too dilute to be plane-destroying, if it went up, but I don't fancy the instrumentation's chance of surviving it.' She glanced directly at Åke. 'Nor a T-suit.'

'But without power, how will we sig—'

'The suits will stay heated – and their power supplies are all sealed, so there's no spark risk there. Good for a couple of days, at any rate.'

'Couple of *days*?' Åke interrupted, incredulous. Why would rescue take a couple of days?

'Fraid so, Oak.'

Without main lighting, the plane's interior became an ill-defined void in which every turn of a helmet's headlamps brought out in relief a streaking judder of harshly-flashed blue-grey surfaces, looming, disconnected. Out of the lamp-glare, the cavernousness shaded to a deep brown, courtesy of the disheartening vista beyond the windscreen.

Åke sat with his mother in the cockpit, staring at the dead control boards and wondering when something *useful* would happen. Beyond the amplified echoing rasp of his own breathing, he could hear the clatter and scrape from outside, as his father made an inspection of the downed Volker, seeking the site of the leak. But Åke's mother said this was a waste of time, by now – even if they sealed it, they couldn't be sure it was safe to reactivate the Volker's systems. The lights would stay off.

The windscreen already seemed darker than it had in the minutes immediately following the crash, only some of which, Åke realised with a shock, was due to a darkening sky, or gathering dust. Part of the windscreen's new-found opacity was caused by a thickening accumulation of water-frost, as the plane's interior cooled towards Titan ambient.

'There's a nasty crack trailing back from one of the underskid nacelles, rear of the left wing,' his father reported to them, back in the cabin after his EVA. His T-suit, which had been regulation lake-placid-blue not an hour ago, was already stained to green and orange-brown around the joints, where flakes of windblown tholin had stuck and smeared. 'I'd say that's your leak, assuming it goes all the way through. And the battery casings have been abraded to hell, and then some. And, Murphy's law, the only live beacons are the underwings, which are next to useless. But aside from that… it could have been a lot worse. Hell of a lot worse. You did good, Junko.'

'Let's just hope they can find the cocking fault. I don't fancy wearing pilot error.'

'Yeah, no, there was clearly something wrong with the plane. It wasn't handling right, in the air. Maybe the rain at Porco got into its electrics, or something, interfered with the main trunk.'

'Like *you're* the cocking expert.' But she said it without apparent malice, for once.

Åke realised, with a start, that his parents were no longer arguing – at least, not in the all-too-familiar sense of words-as-weapons. As though the situation had become too uncertain for that…

'Where are we?' Åke asked. 'Is it too far to just walk home?'

'About fifty kay short,' his mother answered, turning to look out, or rather at, the nearly-opaqued windscreen. 'We're out of Hotei proper, at least. But we fell shorter than I'd hoped. We're just going to have to sit tight.'

'Can we use the suits' radios?' he asked.

'They don't have anywhere near the range, Oak. But we're on course. Someone will spot us, soon enough.'

'You reckon?' Åke's father interjected, looking at his mother. 'You've seen that cloud cover, the sats will be blind in this. And the amount of dust caking the plane, we'll be pretty effectively camouflaged.'

'You have a better idea?'

'I could walk it,' his father said.

'Todd, don't be ridiculous.'

'I'm *not* being ridiculous. It's fifty kay—'

'More like sixty.'

'Alright, sixty. Still, six kay an hour, that's only ten hours, twelve to be generous, allowing for terrain. And there's still days of daylight left.'

'How would you find—'

'I've surveyed all around this area for work. I'll get a bearing from the sun when I set off – it's shrouded, but it should still be visible enough. I won't get lost. And the terrain's not exactly complicated.'

'I want to go too,' Åke announced, quietly.

'Oak, nobody's going *anywhere*. Our flight's been logged. We just need to sit tight and wait for rescue.'

'Junko, can you honestly tell me rescue won't be more than a couple of days away, if we just leave it up to them? Remember when Mitchell's flight—'

'That was *last year*,' she replied. 'The recommendations—'

'—say that first and foremost, parties should be guided by their own common sense. And it took them the best part of a week to get to Mitchell. Goddamn waste, because they could've saved – Look, we can loft a visibility balloon to help pinpoint us. And I can take that canister of trail nuggets for added insurance. I can do this.'

'But *sixty kay*, Todd,' she protested. 'I mean, for cock's sake. And when was the last time you did *anything* in a T-suit? Outside of a sim?'

'Okay, point, but I have simmed twenty in an X-suit. This is lighter.'

'*Simmed*, Todd. Listen to yourself.'

'You got us down here, in close enough to one piece. I couldn't have done that. But I *can* do this. Let me do my bit.'

'This is stupid. Cock, Todd. You really do not need to do this.'

'Yes. Yes, I do.' He lifted an arm as though to make some gesture, stared at his glove, and lowered it again.

'I don't like it,' Åke's mother said. 'Not one cocking bit.'

'Hell, who does?' his father responded. His mother stayed silent, and it dawned on Åke that she'd allowed his father to win this one.

His father grunted again and moved off toward the airlock.

Åke helped his mother with the outer airlock hatch, and then followed her back to the cockpit, to sit and wait. They'd over-pressured the fuselage with spare nitrogen, again, before they'd cracked the now-futile seal, but even so, some more of Titan had inevitably leaked in, dust and taint, before they'd succeeded in closing it again. The air within the cabin, within the cockpit, was already poisoned, but pulling the lock closed would delay the escape of the plane's dwindling warmth.

They were stuck in their suits for the duration, several hours at the very least. And the Volker was going to need decontamination, after, if it was ever going to fly again. Not that that was his problem, or his mother's: it was just a rental, after all.

Åke suddenly realized one of the implications of being stuck in the suit for an indefinite period. *Gross.* And then, of course, the need to go started steadily to build.

His father, outside, spent several minutes on a reconnaissance around the downed plane's tail section, deploying the Broadwing's visibility balloon. He wiped most of the dust and gunk off the windscreen, unannounced – Åke was momentarily startled by the apparition, eerie light-blue glove smearing across the glass, then disappointed that, through so many layers (his own visor, the still-dirty windscreen, his father's helmet) he couldn't see his father's face with sufficient clarity to make out his expression. Åke waved uncertainly, and his dad raised an arm in reply.

'Well.' He stood maybe five metres ahead of the Volker's nose, waiting. A shape in visibility-blue plastic, an awkward mannequin.

'Godspeed. Todd. Tread safely.'

He didn't reply directly; not to her, except maybe via a grunt. 'Åke? Look after your mother, okay?'

'Bye. Dad.'

Low gravity, the near-opaque windscreen; it didn't take long before his father's servo-boosted strides had taken him beyond sight. Åke shifted back into the co-pilot's seat, the backtank refusing to allow him any comfort. The landscape outside was an unchanging dark sepia, shading to dull tangerine where the prevailing ice had been more recently exposed. Sand, boulders, outcrops, under high thick cloud. The vista was punctuated only by the pitiful bright blue dots of the trail nuggets his father had dropped as he walked: Åke could see one clearly, a second just, maybe a third. They looked far too small to achieve anything useful. Or to offer meaningful security in a landscape likely riven with the hidden killers of Titanian geography: crevasses, subsurface voids, and thinly-crusted pockets of brine. Sixty kilometres was suddenly a much larger distance than it had been a few minutes ago. It would only take one servo-boosted misstep...

Something crawled into the pit of Åke's stomach. Whatever it was, it seemed to be looking for a place to settle. But it would not lie still.

'Idiot. Stupid, stubborn *fool*.'

Åke looked up. He hadn't really been drowsing off. 'Huh?'

'Sorry, Oak. Didn't mean to wake you.'

He wiped some frost from the windscreen. The cloud had darkened, if anything, but nothing else in the view outside had shifted. Not even, it seemed, the slightly fainter patch in the sky that was either the sun, or a pale mark on the screen. 'I wasn't—' He shifted in his seat, again.

His mother was still sitting bolt upright. It had been, Åke was sure, at least an hour since his father had left, and the strain in her face – even seen through the visor – was painful. He reached across, took her gloved hand in the clumsy grip of his own glove, and said, 'It'll be alright, Mum. He'll make it right.'

She squeezed back. 'Thanks, Åke. It's good of you to say that.'

'How much longer d'you think it'll be?'

'I don't want to set a time limit, Oak.'

'What happened with Mitchell's flight?'

'Why don't you play one of your sims?'

'Jeez, Mum. You don't *play* a sim, you *do* it.'

'Alright, then, why don't you—'

'Finished it already, near enough. It'd got boring anyway.'

'Going to get plenty more boring, just sitting here watching nothing.'

'It's alright. What happened with Mitchell's flight?'

She released her son's hand, reached round to the back of her neck, pressed on the seam between the suit's torso and helmet, and lifted her head as though she had a crick.

'Mum?'

'Yes? What, Oak?'

'When I'm an adult, I'm going to be a freight pilot, like you.'

'What, not an analyst like your father? The credit's more.'

'Piloting's more interesting.'

'I don't see how you can say that. I *crashed* you, on your first flight. Second. It's a lot safer, working in a lab.'

'You got us down safely.'

She didn't answer, and after a while he turned in his seat, to look at her. The headlamp's glare, the curved visor: it was difficult to see her face.

He took her hand again, and squeezed, harder this time. And after a minute or so, her breathing became steadier.

Åke had resolved, as his own rescue-effort contribution – his mother had got the plane down, his father had gone off for help – to keep guard, to maintain a vigil. Even if it meant he had to stare out the windscreen at the same patch of ground for a day, he'd do it. To maximise their chances;

to will his father into reappearing, coming closer. Staying safe.

He'd dozed off.

Jerked awake, cotton-mouthed, dull headache just beneath the skin of his temple. But the view, once he'd wiped away the frost, was unchanged. Brown, messy, interrupted by the improbable blue blips of the two, or just maybe three, trail nuggets.

'Don't want to *die* here,' his mother said, suddenly. Strange intonation, as though she was imitating the stilted voice of another.

He'd turned to her in panic. 'Sorry,' she said, a touch embarrassed. 'The music I've been listening to. I think that's enough for now.' She pressed a control on her wrist, leaned back stiffly. Coughed.

'Still not back,' Åke complained.

'It's only been four – no, five hours, Oak,' she said. 'He won't even be *there* yet.'

He waited, to see if she was going to say more, but she didn't. 'It'll be alright, Mum. It will.'

'Oh, he's fit enough. And he says he knows the terrain, which I guess he should. I just do *not* like the look of those clouds. But it's kept from raining, it looks like, touch wood.'

Rain was rare, but it wasn't something to joke about. A methane flood could be frightening. Particularly out here in the open, their only refuge this dead plane.

Up close, the floodplain they'd landed on was lumpy, knobuled with the residue of ancient cryovolcanic flows, and toffee-stained except for the broad line of pale ice, scraped almost clean, that marked the path the Volker's fuselage had scratched across the plain's surface. The ground at the plane's nose was piled with chunks of ice-muck, some of them large as his helmet. Crouching down, picking up a loftball-sized globe of ice, he strove to imagine the landing as it might have been for the plane, rather than for its occupants. He stood up, looked around. It began to seem a little more miraculous, a little less of a given, that they'd survived;

that they were broadly intact.

He strode as far as he dared from the plane. Not in the direction his father had taken, but opposite, so he wouldn't be tempted. From a couple of hundred metres away, the Volker became insignificant; Åke was alone on Titan. It struck him that the terrain out here was different to that around the settlements, in a way he should have expected but hadn't: no antennae, no beacons, no landscape engineering. A wilderness, in a sense that made the open space surrounding Solà, as innately lethal as any stretch of ground on the world's surface, seem tame and almost artificial by comparison. The sense of distance, of danger, spooked him, and for a panicked moment, turning back towards the plane, he could not see it where he'd expected to. He retraced his steps, breathing quickly, ashamed at how easily he'd almost lost himself.

It was an unequal contest. The world was too big. Everything was so cramped, in the settlements, and yet there was all this *space* out here. A trap.

The ground behind the Broadwing sloped, a little. If there was enough rain – if there was a flood, if things went beyond control, it'd come from *that* direction, down the slope, towards the plane.

A trap. If there was a flood – he allowed the concept to take root, so as to savour the idea – he'd have to *do something* to protect the plane, which was vulnerable here within the slight dip it had settled in. The idea thrilled him, quickened his pulse.

But protect it how? The Broadwing was much too bulky for one or even two people to drag to higher ground, even if he dialled the T-suit's augments up to maximum. Or he could put an obstacle in the flood's path, pile up ice, slush and rubble to make a sort of dam, a breakwater or whatever they called it; but he didn't think they had anything on the Volker that would help with that. And a flood could also put his father, still somewhere out amidst the wastelands between here and Solà, in danger. He allowed the iceball to drop from his hands, stared at the stain its melt had left on his T-suit gloves.

It would be best if there was not a flood. If it did not rain.

Both unsettled and disappointed by this, he knocked on the airlock door, signalling to his mother that he was ready to come back in. They manhandled the lock open between them. It seemed to have grown more resistant, possibly with gunk accumulating within the lintel, and did not want to close again.

He was back in the cabin, back in the co-pilot's seat.

'This isn't your fault,' she said. At least, he *thought* she'd said it, but he couldn't clearly remember the sound of the words. He had been dozing a little, again. It was difficult to tell how much time had passed. He made a small noise, somewhere between a 'Huh?' and one of his father's grunts, but she didn't amplify her remark. So he remained unconvinced.

He wiped the windscreen, looked out, tried to regain the sense of *vigil*. But the spell, or the need, or some component of his self-promise had come adrift, and it would not work.

Had he failed somehow? Would his father, now, not show? The weight of the responsibility was an ache, in his throat, in his gut, somewhere he couldn't reach. He should have kept watch. 'Mum?'

She coughed a couple of times, dry, awkward noises, and took a sip from her helmet's water-teat before responding. Her voice still sounded rough. 'What is it, Acorn?'

It had been years since she'd used that nickname. And he realised, now, he didn't know what to ask her, because he hadn't mentioned the vigil out loud. 'Uh – how long did you have to fly for the company, before they let you handle the Lufters?'

'Huh. I just had to sit another licence. But they'll probably have something newer, faster, if you – by the time you get to be a pilot.'

'That'd be cool.'

She turned, in her seat, towards him. 'You know, a Lufter wouldn't have made this flight any real amount faster,' she said. 'And it would have been rougher. Well, except for the last bit, of course.'

'How's that?'

'Lufters are designed to fly in the interwind,' she said.

'I know *that*, Mum.'

'Yes, but to get that high – sixty, seventy klicks – you've got to climb a long way through steepening winds. A short hop like this, you'd almost only get to the interwind before you needed to go into descent again. The Broadwing's not fast, but it stays low, where everything's calmer. Most of the time. The hairiest – some of the hairiest flying I've ever done has been in a Lufter, making that descent.' She coughed again, from somewhere deep in her belly so that her whole torso shook.

He wanted to ask if they'd let him ride in one, as a passenger, if he stayed out of mischief. But he didn't quite dare, for fear of disappointment. There was enough else wrong at the moment, without that. He was beginning to wish he'd tried to talk his father out of walking away.

It grew cold enough that ice rimed every surface within the aircraft, and even found purchase on the casings of their suits. He pressed the fingertips of his heated gloves against his forearm, and watched the lazy way in which the frosting acquiesced to warmth.

They played I, Spy until they both agreed it was making them fractious. Then she did some more music, and he stared at the trail markers, as though they were magical talismans, until they grew auras for themselves. His mother got up every so often, to go back and check over something in the Volker's rear. Åke, who'd been flirting with sleep for a couple of hours now, finally succumbed. There just wasn't anything else to help keep him awake, not even the pervasive chill.

The vigil had been a stupid idea. As if their situation could possibly be in any way under his control.

He wasn't sure, later, what had disturbed him. Perhaps it was just the overwhelming, thudding need to pee, or the coldness permeating through the limbs of his T-suit. He'd looked up, wondering why his neck had to hurt so bad, cleaned the glass; and noticed that the third trail marker, the most distant, seemed slightly brighter.

Except when he looked again, it wasn't the trail marker. The shape was wrong. And it moved.

Åke turned to his mother, shook her urgently, and found that his throat wouldn't let him speak. He swallowed the lump, pointed out the windscreen, and managed, 'It's Dad! It's Dad! He's back! Mum, he's back!'

'Hm,' she replied, a strange, noncommittal noise, but she sat herself up.

It wasn't his father. But it was coming from the same direction, and it was help.

He hoped they had found his father.

He waited, shot through with impatience, while the broad blue bulk of the rescue crawler slowly scraped across the landscape towards them. It had the look of a five-seater. Not, he eventually decided with mild disappointment, one of the new Hainan All-Terrains. Just a Mitsuda ERV; but it would do.

emptying roesler

It was old enough, now, to have earned the description 'brownstain', and from the outside the building had indeed acquired a darkened, streaked, camouflaged appearance. But, looking around the structure's foyer while he shucked off his T-suit, Niall could imagine that the arcology would have looked impressive, once. The twenty-metre-high atrium was dominated by a central, sand-bedded palm tree which stretched most of the way up to a vaulted 'sky-blue' roof. A gentle double-helix rampway provided access to five storeys of living space. And, not quite the submerged iceberg, there lay somewhere beneath Niall's feet the twenty metres or so of basement plant: reactor, life support, insulation, heating system, and other equipment routinely needed to protect the building's human occupants from the inhospitable extremes of the Titanian environment. In its heyday – a quarter-century or more ago – Roesler would have housed somewhere between thirty and forty families. Aside from the particularity of its central botanical feature, the arcology reminded Niall of the habitat Lib had lived in, with her parents, when he'd started seeing her a decade and a half ago.

But here, now, decay had set in. The palm tree (held erect only by a sturdy polymer-guy latticework straining against its lower trunk) was dead, the building almost so. Apartment hatchways – emergency airlocks – lay open, rooms deserted; some untidily bare, some detritus-filled. Graffiti both static and crudely animated covered just about every available surface, overlaying itself to the extent that very little was naked-eye readable. It would present, Niall thought, an interesting challenge for his augments, but he wasn't in the mood to attempt a decipher. The air was cold, dry, and acrid with the stink of tholin and ammonia, the lighting uneven and yellowed, the flooring disconcertingly sticky and garbage-strewn: Roesler was a dump. It was as good as abandoned.

Except, of course, that in truth it wasn't quite abandoned. Which was where Niall came in.

There were parts of his job that he hated, and this was one of them.

Up on the third level, the floor-littering crud was no longer evident. It was as though the detritus of the lower levels were simply wrack, the waves of which had not reached this height. The walls, too, though hardly pristine, at least showed some evidence of recent attempts at cleaning, the graffiti less dominant. The ammoniacal odour was, if anything, stronger than ever. Niall started taking note of the hatchway numbering. Eighteen… nineteen… Xu was number twenty-seven, apparently. Next level up.

Twenty-seven was a plain white hatchway which looked to have been so recently repainted that Niall was almost reluctant to knock, though he looked in vain for an alert-pad, sensor, or transcom. He doubted, though, that Xu was still ignorant of his presence here. Niall thumbed the butt of his sidearm absently, adjusted the hem of his tunic so as to better conceal the weapon, coughed softly, and rapped his knuckles on the hatchway's thick plastic.

The sound of movement from within. No spoken response.

Niall counted off ten seconds. 'Xu? Mr Jethro Xu?'

More movement, still from deep within the apartment.

He tried again. 'Xu?'

'You pronounce it *Shoo*, not *Zoo*.' A deep voice, cultured and modulated, from somewhere behind the hatchway. Footsteps. The hatchway's door panel slid upwards. Jethro Xu was tall (*one eighty-nine point five*, suggested Niall's augments), slender of frame (*local weight eight point one two kilograms, mass fifty-eight point three*), and dark-skinned (*melanin content on the seventy-ninth percentile, plus or minus two*). His hair was close-cropped, more white than grey, his nose dramatically hooked. He was also dripping wet, and clad only in a towel.

While his eyes skittered up and down the man's torso, Niall wondered absently if the augments' estimate had been a dry weight. 'My apologies,' he began.

'You didn't come all this way to offer those,' Xu responded, at a louder than customarily conversational volume. (Hearing impairment, perhaps? Or just out of practice with speech, these past ten months?) 'Who are you, and what's your business here?'

Niall raised his badge. 'My name is Niall Ranafin,' he said, making an effort to talk loudly and clearly.

'Pol?'

Niall nodded. 'South Sagan.'

'It sure doesn't say 'Ranafin' on that badge,' observed Xu, squinting. Rheumy eyes, though they evidently still worked fine. The augments hadn't volunteered an age estimate, but Niall already knew it from the file. Sixty-two. An *old* sixty-two, Niall thought, judging by those eyes. The health card might be the one to play here, then?

'No. My name's properly Ranafinjanahary, but most people find that a mouthful.'

'I can hardly say mine offers me the luxury of truncation,' countered Xu. 'And I can tell you now, just so you don't wind up wasting more time over this, that I'm not leaving. So you can pass that on to your bosses. Your paymasters.'

'I wish it were that easy, Mr Xu. But I have a responsibility to ensure that this dwelling – this structure is made safe, and it would be negligent of me to disregard that. At least hear me out, please. May I come in?'

'I'll not change my mind.'

'Neither will those you oppose. But I have an interest in attempting to resolve this in an amicable way, if that's possible.'

'Give a man time to get dressed. Come back in ten minutes.'

'I'll just wait,' said Niall. 'Not a lot of scope for sightseeing.'

'That's hardly *my* fault, now, is it?' replied Xu, as the hatch slid closed.

Despite his assertion, Niall found the prospect of a ten-minute sojourn standing at Xu's threshold to be stultifying. He wandered down the ramp in a seemingly-aimless fashion, paying more attention this time to the detritus as he re-entered its realm. Wrappers and dried food scraps accounted for much of it, miscellaneous bits of disposable plastic rubbish – squashed containers, crushed bottles, torn bags, etc – dominated the remainder. There were some household utensils, broken cups, and sadly-dissected toys; pieces of demised furniture; clothing either too old, too worn, or too soiled to have been retained by its owners. A modern-day midden, the rubbish offered enough indications (to anyone who might bear an interest) of what the building's former occupants had prized, by displaying so clearly what they did not.

He was just about to retrace his steps to Xu's hatchway when he saw the phial. Just a round-ended translucent polymer tubule, smaller than any of his fingers. Empty. Upon closer inspection, unsealed, never loaded. The kind of cheap, mass-produced article that was commonplace in a half-dozen licensed pharmaceutical laboratories in this prefecture, and that had no purpose – no legitimate purpose – outside of such a laboratory. Lab workers didn't normally take their work home with them. Of those that did...

Niall's forehead tightened, lips locked shut, breath drawn sharply in through his nose. In delayed reaction – but the phial was *unloaded*, his rational mind reminded him, it could present no possible danger – his heart accelerated.

Pharmhands.

Eight years ago, Niall had lost Lib. After a fashion.

Pharmhands, looking to expand their turf, had unleashed phloo on Brouwer. The habitat's administrators had elected not to pay the ransom which would have secured the vaccine, trusting instead in detailed testing measures and in curfews to curtail the spread of the tailored psychopathogen. The measures failed. When, two weeks later, the time-delayed infection asserted itself, it rapidly became apparent that Brouwer was unprepared for the resulting epidemic, and for an unusually virulent strain of phloo. Twenty-eight died. Of those who survived, many were hospitalised, some never truly recovering from the chronic health problems experienced in the outbreak's wake. Lib, who'd been working in a sector that suffered a major failure of environment systems during the crisis, had almost perished through oxygen deprivation, exacerbated by the hallucination-impaired efforts of first responders themselves ravaged by phloo.

Brouwer's health professionals had done what they could to restore Lib's mental function, once the habitat's condition had been stabilised; they installed several of the new cognitive implants to redress and circumvent the extensive damage to her neural pathways. Her recovery from the edge of brain-death had been substantial, and the clinicians had bandied about terms like 'highly encouraging' as though that made everything all right. But she wasn't the same person, afterwards. She could never be the same person; she'd lost too much, in those crucial minutes of oxygen starvation. And Niall hated himself for distrusting, second-guessing, downgrading the person she'd become.

They were still a couple. But Niall couldn't say any more why that was.

He pocketed the phial, tried to pull the lid shut on those feelings. He still had a job to do here.

It was closer to fifteen minutes than ten. Long enough that Niall's neatly-marshalled arguments, already disturbed at the sight of the phial, had disarrayed further through the additional waiting for Xu to admit him into the apartment.

Xu led him through a short corridor past a sleepchamber and galley into a brightly-lit living area rimmed with shelving – used mostly for neatly piled clothing, though wooden ornaments, framed images, and a few books were also in evidence – and a faux window. The window's display of a typically Titanian vista – a landscape of tall, broad, parallel dunes, curving in a manner suggestive of a section of some highly-magnified fingerprint, beneath the thick murk of a dark orange sky – might or might not have been local, might or might not have been realtime.

Niall was shown the room's solitary chair, in front of a large drafting table. 'I'll just stand,' he said, looking around the room.

Three of the images on the shelves appeared to be of the same young woman: willowy, dark-skinned, long-haired. 'Family member?' Niall asked, pointing at one of the pictures.

'Daughter,' said Xu. 'She's the reason I'm here. The reason I'm not moving.'

Niall waited for an elaboration.

'She needs to know where to find me,' explained Xu.

'I'm sorry, I don't—'

'She left, five years ago, while her mother and I were still together. I haven't heard from her in the last three, I've no idea whether she's still on Titan. But if she decided she needed to find me again, this is where she'd look.'

'Surely she could just look you up?'

'She doesn't trust databases,' said Xu. 'Takes after her father in that respect.'

'If you're concerned – if you'd consider filing a missing person's report...'

'Concerned? No. Disquieted, mainly. But her absence isn't exactly out of character. And no, I don't want to file a report. That'd be the last thing she'd want. Even if I did trust the pol. No offence.'

Niall stared at Xu, completely unsure of what to make of the other's attitude. He was fairly sure that, if he'd had a daughter or son – if that had ever been on the cards with Lib – he'd want to know their whereabouts, particularly after such a long time missing. Of course, there were reasons why one might *not* want such a thing investigated, particularly if one were fearful of what might turn up. But Xu's body language – and heartrate, skin temperature, respiration rate – did not indicate fear, nor any of the markings of guilt, nor of the markings of guilt's concealment. Xu was presenting, so far as Niall and his augments could tell, an unvarnished version of the truth, or what Xu believed to be the truth.

Still, there were questions that needed to be asked, and those questions provided a useful way of building a rapport. 'Mr Xu,' he began. 'Was your daughter – ?'

'Rosa,' Xu prompted.

'Was Rosa involved in any… activities which might be of concern to the pol?'

'Was she a thief, or an activist, or a pharmhand, you mean? No. Quite the opposite.'

'But you've said yourself that you haven't heard from her in five years. A lot can happen in five years. Aren't you the slightest bit concerned?'

'Three years, not five. She left here five years ago, but we kept in touch over the next couple. She's an independent adult, knows her own mind. I trust her judgement. Because – well, what's the alternative?'

The alternative, Niall thought, was actually trying to fathom what had befallen your daughter. In three years, anything might have happened. Titan was beginning to acquire a reputation as the 'murder capital' of the outer Solar System: in an environment at once intensely inhospitable and comprehensively encrusted by a natural patina of organic material, disposal of human remains was almost laughably easy. Plus, of course, the pharmhands. He wondered if it might be worthwhile pursuing his own enquiries, on the quiet, to see what he could learn of Rosa Xu. But the odds were, such queries wouldn't go down well with his superiors: Niall had gained a reputation, at South Sagan, for showing a little too much interest in investigations involving pharmhands, and while there was nothing directly suggesting Xu's daughter might be connected with the gangs, there was always that suspicion surrounding missing-persons cases. Hence here he was, relegated to tackling a situation that could just as well have been handled by a soc worker. Besides, what to tell her father, if it transpired she'd met with foul play? If she'd been grind-and-sprayed, scattered amongst Senkyo's dunes, somewhere between here and Lunine? Particularly after Xu had as good as warned him off.

'I think some degree of concern would be understandable. But as you say, you trust her judgement. I wish all parents could say the same.' The day wasn't getting younger, and this didn't seem to be bringing Xu's compliance forward any. Time for a change of tack. 'I've been wondering whether you have any family connection to Xu Aerospatiale,' said Niall.

'Shona Xu was my father's cousin. And yes, I was a cog in the dynastic machine, for a decade or so. But I was never the corporate type, never the team player.'

'I was starting to get that impression about you, yes,' said Niall.

'Why do you ask?'

'Well, the name, obviously. And,' Niall pointed to one of the wooden objects on the shelf, painted, intricate, and chunky, 'there's that item there. Whatever it is.'

'It's a miniature, a prototype. Never made it to production.'

'I didn't know Xu Aerospatiale were ever looking to diversify into habitats?'

'Oh, it's not a habitat, it's a vessel. A submersible. It didn't work properly, failed on its first, unmanned dive. And Volker got the contract anyway, for something much simpler, just one step removed from a glass-floored boat. Turns out the northern-lakes tourists didn't actually want to dive so much, just to be able to see for a way beneath the surface.'

'And this was your design work?'

'Mr Ranafinjary—'

'Ranafinjanahary. I told you, it's a mouthful. And in all honesty, 'Ranafin' is completely fine with me. Or Niall, if you prefer.'

'Mr Ranafinjanahary. I appreciate that you're here, as you see it, to perform a duty. I'd rather you just stick to that script, and not try to – what? Ingratiate yourself with me? I'm not leaving. And I'd prefer not to waste time on past irrelevancies.'

'As you wish. But I generally find the past is not as irrelevant as you would like to make out.'

66

'Admirably philosophical of you. But please...' Xu turned his wrist, briefly unfolded his fingers in a gesture just one step removed, Niall thought, from a 'pay up' signal.

'Very well,' said Niall. 'You're aware that Wurlingame-Esterfjord, as the arcology's owner, operator, and lessor, want you out by the end of the month?'

'I'm aware of it. I don't agree to it. And I'm not costing them anything. My presence here is not inconveniencing them in the slightest.'

'Not inconveniencing them. How can you *say* that? I'm not privy to – but look, you can't know what their plans for the structure might be.'

'It's a forty-year-old building. Occupancy has fallen away to, well, to just me, because nobody seems to want to live in small communities nowadays. There's no mining any more – sorry, we're supposed to call it primary resource extraction nowadays, aren't we? No industry to speak of around here, this part of the Senkyo. And the site has nothing to recommend it. It's just a white elephant. Only with me here, I can upkeep all the engineering – I don't thank my time with the firm for much, but at least it taught me a useful trade – so the owners get an *occupied* white elephant, a *well-maintained* white elephant, ready for when housing fashions change back, as seems likely, in a decade or two's time. Once this misguided drive towards urbanisation – too many eggs, too few baskets – has run its course.'

'Hang on. You're saying you've been putting in maintenance on the arcology's plant?'

'Yes.'

'It's not your plant,' argued Niall.

'No, that's true. But can you really expect me to believe – do you yourself believe for one moment – that W-and-E are seriously going to excavate it, gut it, and re-use four-decade-old enviro engineering in one of their sleek modern modular builds? It'd cost them more to reclaim the kit than to leave it be, here, and it would never pass licence if they were looking to incorporate it elsewhere. They're not that fucking stupid. They are only doing this because they can, not because it's in anyone's best interests. Not even theirs.'

'But it's *their equipment*. And as the legal owners of Roesler, Wurlingame-Esterfjord are well within their rights to order your eviction. My hands are pretty much tied, Mr Xu. Yours, too, I'm afraid.'

'You might think that. I disagree. Look, this is a still-functional habitat, currently the only hab in at least a four-hundred-klick radius. I've kept the place running, single-handed, for the best part of a year now, haven't been costing W-and-E a jot.'

'Which is pretty much irrelevant in the eyes of the law—'

'Is it? It shouldn't be. I'm providing a service, using a structure nobody else is currently using, and—'

'What 'service' do you mean?'

'Sanctuary. Safe haven. Call it what you like. Say there's an accident, twenty or thirty klicks away. If I'm not here, if Roesler goes derelict, there's just the respite dome on Weathertop, eighty or more klicks away, and God only knows if that's kept Titan out since the last time anyone used it. And after that, Clemence is the nearest actual settlement. If someone needs to go for help, that's a long walk to Clemence, through the thick of dune country. Even with a fully-charged T-suit, you'd never make it. We shouldn't be abandoning places like Roesler. We *need* places like this. Survival's difficult enough on Titan, without actively doing stuff that makes it worse.'

'That would be a matter you'd need to raise with Wurlingame-Esterfjord, Mr Xu. Or, at this stage, with your local political representatives. Meanwhile, my own instructions are clear. The law is clear. You're advised that the habitat's owners have ordered your eviction, and that such eviction will occur on the last day of this calendar month if you do not, voluntarily and of your own accord, vacate the premises before such time. If you require assistance with relocation, the designated agency within South Sagan is—'

'I'm not moving. I suggest you pass that message on to your higher-ups. Will I be seeing you at the end of the month, or will they be sending someone else?'

'Mr Xu... Jethro... you are only making this more difficult for yourself.'

Xu's lip curled, perhaps in offence at Niall's attempt at familiarity. 'I beg to differ. Way I see it, it's Wurlingame-Esterfjord who – ah, shit, look, I've got better things to do with my time, Officer. Why don't you just leave an old man in peace? You've said your bit, I've said mine. The social niceties have been fulfilled.' With that, Xu turned and walked into the galley, not even looking behind him.

As hints went, it was none too subtle. And Niall didn't see any reason, in the circumstances, not to take it.

He heard the hatch's locking mechanism click magnetically into place behind him.

Niall had to remind himself that this wasn't actually trespassing; but it *felt* like it.

The structure was officially derelict; he had been granted full rights of entry and search by the owners, subject only to respecting Xu's privacy. But it was natural enough to see Xu, who had after all taken on *de facto* custodianship of the arcology, as the building's sole occupant. So, while rummaging around in the building's control room was entirely within the discretion Niall had been given, it didn't feel right. It didn't help that the control room, clean, dust-free, and clear of graffiti, also showed signs of decoration – a small wooden figurine and a sketchbook on the workbench – which were unmistakably the work of Xu.

But it wasn't just his own perceived intrusion that seemed amiss. There was something else that didn't tally. Something was wrong here. Jethro Xu had been the sole inhabitant here these last ten months, and was obviously sufficiently houseproud to have not only kept up the minor maintenance required on the habitat's environment engineering, but also to have embarked on the process of cleaning up the building, slowly clearing it of refuse. But...

Niall retrieved from his pocket the phial he'd found in the second-floor garbage. Turned the small tubule over in his hand.

He called up a wall display, spent a few minutes overriding the system's security. Then he started a search back through the foyer's camera records. He flicked past the foreshortened views of his own entry, just an hour or so earlier, and was rewarded with some grainy footage of the intruders, timestamped three weeks previously. There were five of them, all T-suited but with helmets off: two men, stocky, pasty, cropped hair, mid-to-late thirties, and sufficiently alike in appearance that they might as well be brothers; a woman of similar age, tall, dark, shaven head; and two younger women, one tall, sharp-faced, long-haired, the other shorter and rounder. They stood, for a few moments, just inside the entrance airlock. Two of the intruders were carrying large cases, and one of the others – the tall younger woman – held an ambiguously-shaped device, not quite sufficiently streamlined to suggest 'gun', in her left hand. Niall could almost feel his augments itching at the corners of his eyes, impatient to parametrise the images, interpolate heights, record distinguishing characteristics… but he refused the tech's eager anticipation of involvement, deliberately let the opportunity pass. Maybe later. Their bearing – a blend of self-assurance and stealth – told him everything he needed to know about this group.

He watched them move across to the rampway, ascend to the second floor, look in at an empty room. And stop.

The woman with the device turned and pointed it at him – no, not at him, at the camera that had been tracking them, Niall reminded himself – and the vid record stopped abruptly.

And when he gestured to arrange its playback, the imagery seemed no longer to exist.

Pharmhands. The thought inevitably conjured, for him, the face of Lib, the face over which he'd searched these years past, repeatedly, for the deep recognition he'd once found there so readily.

If they'd last broken in less than a month ago, the odds were they'd also visited several other times during Xu's self-imposed solitude. To what end?

Save the one ephemeral sequence he'd seen, the vid record had been cleansed in some manner. A forensic examination of the file might well identify gaps, intervals which would help to pinpoint the timing of any incursions, might even recover that hidden footage; but he didn't have the expertise for that, nor really the patience to make the attempt right now.

Pharmhands didn't sample their own produce; didn't lose focus; didn't lay waste, except to make a deliberate example. They didn't litter, didn't vandalise; it was beneath their ambitions, and might well offer forensic clues as to where they had been before, perhaps hints of where they'd move next. Pharmhands didn't do anything without purpose, without a point. But amongst the mess left by the building's former occupants, the dropped phial was a mistake which had gone unnoticed and uncorrected.

What would pharmhands want with a messy, almost-vacant arcology? Their long-term security rested on the need for seclusion: they made their homes in disused mineshafts, unregistered vehicles, small temporary dwellings. Always transitory, except for those of their number who led double lives, secret lives in large cities (like Sagan) where a degree of anonymity was attainable.

A completely empty building, still drawing power from its reactor, still radiating warmth to the cryonic Titanian environment, would draw considerable suspicion, and would not long evade investigation. An *almost-*empty building, however, would clearly need to be kept warm, so as to keep its sole occupant alive… Such a building would be the perfect place to conceal something which might require warmth and a carefully-controlled environment. Something that was at once of exceptional value and deeply incriminating. Something deadly dangerous, something worth hiding.

Niall left the control room, strode along the corridor, down the rampway. He threw a glance into each open hatchway he passed, assessed the level of mess within each abandoned apartment. Down on the second level, two doorways along (if his memory was correct) from where he'd found the phial, he found the apartment they'd stopped at. Number Eleven. It was locked shut, but Niall had been issued with the master keys, just in case.

He thought, straight away, that he must have got it wrong, because the room was messy with abandoned household rubbish. The detritus was thickest in what would have been the living-space, but it was in the bedroom that he found what they'd hidden. A wardrobe, door barely ajar and banked by a deep drift of discarded clothing. The back wall of the wardrobe was a close match to the rest of the room's surfacing, but it didn't fool Niall's augments. Behind the false wall there stood an incubator rack, broad and almost as tall as Niall himself. The rack, its telltales all green, contained hundreds upon hundreds of filled and sealed phials...

It would need careful handling. The pharmhands would surely know about the clearance order for the arcology, would know that it was scheduled to be evacuated and powered down within the next two weeks. They would almost certainly be back to claim their harvest, remove all traces, before then.

If he reported it back up the chain, as would be expected of him, matters would be taken out of his hands. An operation would be mounted, which might or might not lead to the capture of pharmhands: without knowledge of the gang's day-to-day plans, it would be necessary to maintain surveillance over the trackway leading to the arcology, and such external surveillance could all too easily draw attention to itself. A self-powered monitoring installation, somewhere in the landscape nearby, would leak infrared like a beacon; a manned vehicle or temporary hab-dome, sitting idle out in the Senkyo dunefields would be considerably more conspicuous again. And there was every chance, assuming the pharmhands were as tech-savvy as the disappearing vid record suggested, that they would be monitoring their prize in some manner. A probe, a relay, a bug: such things would be easy to conceal among the refuse in these rooms. They might well already know that he had found their trove, if they had something piggybacked onto Roesler's transmission grid.

The pharmhands could be back within hours, particularly if they had learnt of Niall's explorations. Whereas it would take the best part of a day for South Sagan to properly organise surveillance for the arcology, and to begin to move assets into place.

Was it a matter, he wondered, of necessarily doing the right thing, or could a case be made, sometimes, for choosing instead the least bad wrong thing?

It was a question he'd pondered, often, these past eight years.

He began piling up as much discarded clothing as he could find, spilling it onto the wardrobe floor, and trailing it across the room into the living-space.

He thumped on the hatchway panel, a fast, urgent rhythm. It would be just his luck if Xu was the kind to nap. 'Mr Xu! Mr Xu! Jethro!' The smoke in the corridor was getting thick – perhaps he'd overdone it with the accelerant? But he'd needed the fire to be intense, particularly when it penetrated into the wardrobe, so as to ensure thorough incineration of whatever the incubator rack had contained. Apartment Eleven, by now, was one big smoky fireball, surplus smoke billowing out and up into the atrium. Niall's eyes stung. He'd have expected the fire-suppression system to have activated well before this. 'Mr Xu!'

The hatch slid apart. 'What do—' Xu began, then took a breath, coughed as the air's acridity reached his nostrils.

'We need to evacuate, *now*,' said Niall, hefting his helmet. 'You have your T-suit handy?'

'Of course. But – you did this. You started this. You must have, or you wouldn't have still been here.'

'I needed to complete my report,' said Niall. 'And I smelled smoke. It's coming from down below, second level somewhere. We don't have long.'

Xu stared, eyes narrowed, full into Niall's eyes, and a deep frown developed on the older man's face. 'My life is here. And I don't see any reason why I should be following you anywhere. You started this! I never thought W-and-E would sink so low.'

Niall coughed, turned briefly away. The smoke in the atrium was now thicker than it had been moments before, and he could feel his augments straining to analyse it. Damn things didn't help at times like these. 'We don't have time to argue. We need to get clear of the structure. My flyer's just outside. Get your suit and follow me.'

'I'm not—'

'Staying here is not an option now,' Niall interrupted, with a bluntness that surprised himself.

Something passed across Jethro Xu's face. His brow creased as he threw a glance over Niall's shoulder, at the smoke. 'Wait here.' He turned and walked quickly into his apartment, leaving the hatch opened.

Niall waited just seconds before following the other man into the apartment. Xu ignored him, moved into the bedroom, took an empty case out of his wardrobe, then returned to the living-space. '*T-suit*, I said,' Niall reminded him, moving to grab the case.

Xu shook him off, glared. 'Give me a minute. You bastard.' Niall decided not to push too hard, retreated towards the corridor. If this was the price of his compliance…

Xu placed the case on his drafting table, opened it, and ransacked his shelves with an efficiency that Niall found disconcerting. Several wooden carvings, the framed pictures, a few books: that was all. He spent a few moments in contemplation of the objects remaining on the shelves, breathed deeply, and sealed the case shut, still only half full. 'Right.'

'Your T-suit—' Niall said, turning his attention back from the building's cavernous stack of roiling smoke, as the other man walked back towards him. Xu stopped in the galley's entryway and took a tarnished, sharp-smelling T-suit and helmet out of a closet. Niall helped him step into the body of the suit and checked that its neck-flange assembled properly in readiness for the helmet.

'You *bastard*,' Xu repeated, cradling his suit's helmet. 'I told her I'd be here, if she ever needed me. How's she going to find me now?'

Niall remembered the willowy girl of Xu's pictures, the tall dark woman he'd fleetingly seen on the control-room screen. Wished, now, that he'd let his augments kick in after all. Not that it would have made anything simpler. Sometimes it was better not to know.

How long was too long to wait?

'It's been three years,' he replied, angry at the tears trying to leak out. 'Three years. She's had her chance.'

Xu pushed past him, pressing him quite roughly against the doorway's frame, then heading for the rampway, not caring to look back. Niall lifted his helmet into place and followed.

Too little, too late, the building's sprinklers finally activated.

crevjack

'Suit's overheating.' Lex's voice, low, laboured, rattling in her earpiece.

Probably not so much the suit, love, Teresa Maria commented to herself, as she shepherded them through the unfamiliar, false-coloured nightscape revealed by their helmets. Boots crunched, step after step, along the tacky edge of the newly-gouged trench: a dirty-ice surface, like much of Titan's terrain hereabouts, but at least the freshly-scraped ice made for reasonably sure footing, and for steady, stealthy progress towards their goal.

It made sense, though, that the problems would start with Lex. Of the four, Lex was the most sedentary, the least fit, least able to shrug off the fact that Dayani's improvised nightsuits more than doubled their mass. *A little more time training in an X-suit, you wouldn't be sweating as much now.* 'Take a shot. And, hon, cut the chatter.' But it had been difficult for Teresa Maria, when Dayani and the kid had first brought the idea to her, to see how she could be involved, and not include Lex. The impulse had been, all through the past year, to include him in everything she did. And she did, very much, enjoy his company, his companionship: he was easy to be around, attentive, kind-hearted. She'd often told him he brought out the best in her.

Yet for present purposes, Lex's presence could well turn into liability. If they hadn't needed his flyer…

'But if the comms are secure—' Cory cut in on Teresa Maria's reverie. His voice was higher-pitched than Lex's, more reedy.

Cory's problem, she predicted, would not be fatigue: it would be nervousness. Well, she doubted that any of them were immune to that at the moment. *And you should know not to trust the comms, kid.* 'Still no sense risking it. Halt.'

How much further, to the warm thing?

Teresa Maria needed to take a shot herself. She paused, turned, and lifted her right arm. It took a split second for the grainy imagery, playing on the screen of her nightsuit's visor, to catch up with the change in her motion: a disorienting distraction. She was acutely conscious of the sound of her breathing, her heartbeat, the rustle of the suit's not-especially-supple layers, all of it loud and confining in her ears. Frequency-multiplied in her helmet's heads-up display, the trench's scraped-ice floor glowed a pale and sickly orange where it was warmest, fading elsewhere to dull crimson, then ruddy brown; the rest of the vista, the low hills on the eastern horizon and the more pronounced peaks to the south, were visible only in ghostly silhouette against the yet colder sky. The suits of her three companions were mere silhouettes also, only discernible as ill-defined intrusions on the skyline: bulked-up, balloonish caricatures of the human form. *One hundred and eighty-seven below, and we don't show against the terrain. Not even the visors. Dayani's done well with the suits.*

Teresa Maria aimed – as best she could – back down the trench, well away from the uncertain shapes of the other three. She felt the servos whine in her sleeve, nudging her arm to alignment with an arbitrarily-chosen point just below the horizon. *Target acquired,* her visor advised. She screwed her eyes shut and gave her sleeve's laser the command for the cooling shot.

'Were we expecting company?' Dayani asked.

Teresa Maria blinked her eyes open and glanced around, her arm and side still stinging with the sudden cold, then noticed that Dayani was watching the sky. She looked up. It took a couple of seconds before she could make it out. *Shit.* Atop everything else, her promise to her long-dead younger sister rammed home, hard. 'We've still got time,' she said to the others, though she feared they didn't. 'Move it.'

*

Things had been good, in Ponnamperuna. They were no longer good.

The elevator, though not yet an actuality, had changed the world's financial topography. Ponnamperuna had been well-situated on the northwestern skirts of Xanadu, a convenient home for the brineminers, the muckminers and the carbon-foundry workers, the designers, technicians, culturefarmers and cryonists whose products had found ready export to the bustling arcologies of Kuiper, some three thousand klicks to the southwest, or southeast to the aerospace factories and launch facilities of Woltjer. Ponnamperuna *made sense*, on a world where produce was hurled above the thick atmosphere by means of chemical rocketry; but that world was fading, as the promise of the elevator brightened like an incandescent thread. In the tomorrow of the elevator, Sagan would hold sway, and all of the heavy industries were already rushing to relocate, seeking prime position close to the skyward column. Around Ponnamperuna, there were few left but the culturefarmers, and who – other than a small number of stubborn designers, some artisan types, and the settlement's residual elderly – would the culturefarmers feed? Prices were kept fixed, even while incomes were in freefall. It was a scenario playing out all over Titan's far side, but from what Teresa Maria had heard, Ponnamperuna had it worse than most.

It looked set to get worse yet, too. Teresa Maria and her friends had stuck it out too long in Ponnamperuna. Waiting for a regional resurgence that, it was now evident, was never going to occur; they had left it too late to be able to afford relocation.

If they wanted luck, they'd need to make it for themselves.

She had doubted the kid's self-vaunted ability to pull off the flightsystems hack, but that wasn't the problem. Cory had coaxed the bird down, sweet as could be.

She'd had concerns, too, about being able to spot the CREV within the kilometres-broad expanse of the improvised drop zone; but that wasn't the problem, either. The Cargo Re-Entry Vehicle had gouged a long, straight furrow across the crud-caked, wind-sculpted ice, the scar still warm in infra-red. The CREV's landing skids hadn't deployed, of course – there were limits to Cory's wizardry – but Teresa Maria thought it unlikely that the husk of the vehicle had been damaged beyond repair. And its contents should be impervious, or close enough.

No, the problem – and she didn't yet know how much of a problem it might be, because a lot depended on whether it was legit, or otherwise – was the dirigible. Stealthed, it still had enough of an IR signature for rangefinding. It was still about five klicks away from the CREV, heading unmistakeably towards it, and moving faster than she'd first thought.

We should have had more time to plan, to rehearse, she thought, crimping the nightsuit's water nipple between her teeth, sucking in a shot's worth of blood-warm water, and swallowing. *But the schedule was what the schedule was. It was now, or not at all.*

She scaled a small hump – something in the trench's substratum which had refused to yield to the CREV's careening bulk a half hour ago – and was rewarded with a glimpse of their prize. Not just the glow of it, but the actual straight-sided block of it embedded in a mucky-ice drift of its own making, not two hundred metres ahead of them now. Still several minutes' walk, in their cumbersome suits.

So close. But they'd left their camo-tarped flyer almost two klicks behind them, so as not to show up on any milsat monitoring of the impact site, while they'd waited for CREVfall. And with the blimp closing...

Lex's voice cut into her thoughts. 'Treem, this looks like more than we'd bargained for. Shouldn't we abort?' he asked.

And give up our best shot at bankrolling the shift to Sagan? Lex, we need this, you and I. But she knew full well he had a point. And it was natural that the others would be looking to her for guidance here. She was the one with security exp, marksmanship credentials, and the ruthlessness to act when action was crucial; they were just workers: miners, technicians. Out of chances, taking a desperate risk.

She was damned if she'd just let the dirigible's occupants scare them off the prize: their prize, Cory's, Lex's, Dayani's. Hers. But there was obviously a place for prudence too, and a need to protect those who were relying on her. And to honour her promise to Ramona. 'We split up,' she said, and paused to take a sip. 'Dayani, you're with me. Lex, you and Cory head back to the flyer. If you can get it to the CREV before that blimp reaches it, fine. But no heroics otherwise – stay safe, stay hidden, wait it out.'

'But you'll be—' said Lex.

'We've got the suits,' Teresa Maria replied, reining in her crowd-control voice with some difficulty. 'We'll be fine. The blimp's after the CREV, not us. Probably don't even know we're here, and I aim to keep it that way.'

'Why Dayani?' Cory asked, an accent of resentment in his tone. 'You'll still need to crack the CREV's casing, you'll need me for that.'

What I need, kid, is to keep you out of harm's way. But, of course, to admit that would be an invitation to open rebelliousness. 'We've got your codes already. And Dayani knows the suits,' she said. 'If it comes to a firefight—'

'Firefight?' Lex asked. 'You say 'stay safe', and now you're talking firefight?'

'I'm *still* saying stay safe, hon. I'm just thinking if push comes to shove – but we don't have time to waste. You guys need to get back, or this won't fly.' *Please, love, don't fight me on this. I don't want to lose either of you. And, frankly, I don't need the distraction.* 'No heroics, remember? Let the suits do what they're best at. Day, you up for this?'

'Point me at them,' Dayani replied, her voice a little too enthusiastic for Teresa Maria's comfort.

The nightsuits, Dayani's handiwork, were a bit of a kludge. All up, they were heavier and far bulkier than a standard T-suit. But whereas a T-suit would leak sufficient warmth to glow like a ghost in infra-red – worst was the visor – the makeshift nightsuits, overengineered with internal refrigeration, did not. It wasn't mil quality, but it wasn't far off, either. In the darkness of a farside Titan night, Teresa Maria was as good as invisible.

She was heating up again, though; an inevitable result of the heat pumps' shepherding of body warmth away from the suit's outer surface. Another millisecond pulse from the cooling UV-A laser would relieve the discomfort, would give her sweat glands respite, but she deferred. Her unease at the approaching dirigible, less than two klicks now, persuaded her to hold fire, for the moment.

Were they mil, or pol, or pharmhands up there? The law, in one form or another, would perhaps not be so bad – it'd be difficult to make off with any of the CREV's valuable cargo of asteroidal ore, but she and Dayani should be able to beat a tactical retreat, if all else failed. They'd lose the opportunity for profit, but they'd live. But if it was pharmhands…

'You got it yet?' she asked Dayani, the other crouching like a swollen caricature in front of the CREV's containment release panel.

'Give me another two,' Dayani said. 'The gloves aren't so brilliant for this.'

'Day, I don't think we have another two. Blimp's closing.'

But it wasn't dropping towards a landing, which puzzled her… until she noticed three smaller objects, dark, hard-edged, falling from the craft's gondola.

They're rappelling, she realised.

And the dirigible was still too far back from the CREV for a troop-drop to make sense. Unless, of course, they had detected the flyer's concealing night-tarp…

As if on cue, an IR-bright searchlight on the gondola's underside – a heat lamp, designed to shine up objects in its path – bloomed into harsh existence, highlighting the rappellers' descent.

Teresa Maria, watching from the helplessness of distance, felt the anguish solidify within her. *Please*, she entreated. *No heroics.*

'Got it,' said Dayani, the tone of accomplishment evident as she lifted the panel aside. 'You gonna help me load the pallet?'

'Day,' replied Teresa Maria, keeping her eyes on the approaching heat lamp, 'we need to go.'

'One minute,' insisted Dayani, starting to lean into the CREV's interior as the area around her brightened gradually. 'Then I'll be right wi—'

There was a jolt, and a low-pitched thud that was loud even through Teresa Maria's suit's insulation. Then something solid struck her suit sleeve, and she jerked away even before she realised it was part of Dayani.

Heart pounding, skin burning, brow crawling with sweat, she risked another glimpse over the bank of rock-hard ice. *Clear.*

At least the terrain didn't present too many difficulties. Cory had brought the CREV down in a region almost free of ice-boulders and other rubble, though there was a fair smattering of low, wind-sculpted hillocks ranging in height from three to ten metres. Teresa Maria was glad of the hillocks, of the opportunity to stay concealed. *If we'd chosen a flatter landing site for the CREV, I'd be dead now.*

She'd put fifty metres or so between herself and the CREV; between herself and the four additional intruders who had been the dirigible's second wave of rappellers. There was no chance now of salvaging anything from the craft. Her focus had to be on getting back to the flyer, and hoping Lex and Cory had not met the fate which had befallen Dayani. *At least it was quick.*

Problem was, those fifty metres were in exactly the wrong direction. She could cut across the still-cooling trench, risking detection as a dark, cold silhouette against the warmer terrain. Otherwise, she'd need to make a wide berth around the CREV, and the plundering pharmhands, at the trench's terminus.

Quickest is best, Teresa Maria told herself, her cheeks and chest aflame. *With luck, their attention will be elsewhere.*

But they'd never believe Dayani had been out here alone. They'd be looking for her; and, while the suit was IR-stealthed, it wasn't exactly camo'd: it would still show in visible. Nor could she be sure that it would withstand the heating effect of the blimp's searchlight beam, holding station above the CREV. She needed to stay well out of that beam.

Four against one. Plus however many there are still on the blimp – call it another half-dozen, maybe – plus the three back towards the flyer. And they're armed with explosive projectiles... while what do I have?

Body heat.

Concentration was already difficult, her head throbbing with suit-induced fever. She'd need to take a shot, very soon, else the suit would just keep pushing her heat back towards her, to the point of heat-stroke. But the cooling laser's pulse, or more properly its bright afterglow, might as well advertise her presence in neon light. Even if she aimed it at the ground, there'd still be reflections.

The technology that was keeping her concealed, by hoarding her heat, was going to kill her; unless she did something about it.

May as well make it count. She dialled the pulse energy to maximum, crimped the pulse duration down to as few picoseconds as the suit's controls would allow, and took careful aim at the dirigible's searchlight. *Target acquired.* Closed her eyes tight, on the HUD's half-second warning.

The adapted mining laser in her sleeve did its thing.

The laser's UV-A pulse, in the high-terawatt range, was itself perfectly invisible. But there was still a flash, even through closed lids: a flightpath aurora, carving a brief beam between laser and target. Then the chill, as the laser's discharge took its thermal toll on her arm. She opened her eyes. There was a satisfying burst of light from the gondola's underside, and then the landscape darkened substantially. She'd overloaded their lamp. She sidled a few paces, in case she'd been spied in the searchlight's deathglow. After a few more seconds, her arm stung with cold so severe she worried, for a moment, that she would pass out...

... but at least, she thought while she strove to pump some warmth back into her arm, *the searchlight's failure should give the pharmhands something else to think about.*

Heat and chill at war within her body, she risked the ungainly lope across the trench, openly panting in fear, waiting every second for the life-ending thud of an explosive projectile into her suit.

*

She'd made good time. But she didn't dare hope yet. There was still a klick or so to go, and her luck couldn't hold indefinitely.

It didn't. Topping the ridge, once again hot from her exertions, she saw the figure – *T-suit, gun, not one of us* – an instant before it apparently 'saw' her, a vague silhouette against the sky. She dropped and rolled instinctively, sought as quickly as possible to get to low ground, away from the traitorous sky. She scrabbled five or six metres away from the spot, before a belated concern at the noise of her movement, and the questionable abrasion-resistance of Dayani's makeshift engineering, pulled her up to a panicked, heart-thumping halt. Still prone, she lifted her gaze from the tholin-crusted ice beneath her. The T-suited figure, some thirty metres distant, glowed blue and green in her visor's false-colour display. It was still staring back and aiming in the general direction of where she'd been; not where she was now. *Thank fuck they're using thermal vision*, she thought. *If they were using visible-range, I'd be screwed.*

There was a bloom of light, somewhere just over the horizon. In the direction of the flyer.

Ramona will never forgive me if…

But her sister was dead, had been for almost a decade. As dead, now, as Dayani, though there'd been nothing quick about the cancer's assault on Ramona's defences…

There's been enough death today. Though even as she told herself this, she knew it wasn't true. Where there was a gun, there would be death.

Was she hot enough yet?

Only one way to find out. She lifted her arm, sighted towards the T-suit's visor.

Blink. Flash. Chill.

Through tears of pain, she watched as the nameless pharmhand flailed – blinded, probably burned, faceplate neatly pierced – and crumpled, knees bending, arms still thrashing as it twisted and pitched backwards toward the ground.

*

She felt sickened, physically nauseated as well as disgusted with herself. There'd been enough of his face left to indicate that the kid in the T-suit had probably not even been Cory's age.

But at least now she had a gun.

What was it they called it? 'Packing heat'?

Running, panting, all thought of stealth now past, she tried to put the pharmhand's face out of her mind. Frequency-multiplied imagery bounced confusingly on the visor's viewscreen, out of synch with the *now* of the terrain. Lactic acid stung in her shins and thighs.

She strained to get more speed out of the sluggardly nightsuit, aware that any stumble, even in Titan's one-sixth-g and with all the suit's high-tech padding, would likely be fatal. She was well aware, too, of the target she must present, plainly cameo'd against the night sky, if another pharmhand happened to peer over the ridge ahead, or around that knoll. But she'd been spooked by that nimbus of light she'd glimpsed a few minutes earlier. She had to get to the flyer, to check whether Cory and Lex were in danger.

Topping the ridge, she took in several things quickly. Eighty metres away, the flyer's skeletal frame was exposed, its night-tarp strewn on the ground beside it. A T-suited figure lay motionless near the flyer; a nightsuited shape, stealth mode apparently failed, sat slumped against the flyer's left rear skid. And a fight was in progress, as the remaining pharmhand grappled with a nearly-invisible opponent. *Cory.* Her blood raced, her duty burned, and almost without thinking she raised the gun, aimed, and fired at the pharmhand.

The gun didn't co-operate.

Neither, a few moments later, did the laser in her suit's sleeve.

Are you fucking kidding me? she thought, dropping the gun and starting to run towards the melee, impeded, as always, by the suit. But she had only covered half the distance when the T-suiter pushed the other face-forward to the ground, planted a boot on his back, and bent down to activate the emergency-release clasp on the nightsuit's air supply. Teresa Maria, still closing, watched in horror as the pharmhand held aloft the precious module, ripping its connection hose off, while Cory squirmed on the ground.

Peripheral vision wasn't brilliant in a T-suit. The suit's occupant noticed Teresa Maria's approach far too late, started to turn.

Momentum carried Teresa Maria into the T-suit, hard. Her right arm, raised as if to shield her chest, slammed across the pharmhand's visor as they connected. The visor shattered, the T-suited woman fell back, her face a barely-glimpsed mask of instant terror. Teresa Maria dodged the unseeing, desperate grasp of gloved hands, steadied her balance, then turned to pick up the ruined oxygen-supply module.

Useless. She threw it aside.

At her feet, Cory still twitched.

Visual, she whispered to her suit. *Stealth off. Lights.* Her headlamps activated. The world suddenly drained of false colour.

Cory's movements on the ground filled her with dread. She turned away, the breath loud in her ears, sharp in her throat.

The spasming pharmhand's T-suit was a Hainan model, off-the-shelf; but the nightsuits were kludged, their fittings non-standard. The Hainan's tanks wouldn't fit. Her nephew would die.

Bile soured her mouth. She felt weak, dizzy. But there was no opportunity to pause. She fumbled, futilely, feverstruck, around the sides, lower back, and shoulders of her own suit, finding nothing useful to grip onto. *No time. No time!*

Heart hammering, adrenaline clamouring, *do something, anything,* she raced to the flyer, to where Lex lay supported by the skid's strut. She'd thought him dead, too. But though there was a nasty breach visible below the suit's left knee, he stirred as she approached. The suit's auto-tourniquet function must have done its job, for once. Her breath caught, and tears pricked at the corners of her eyes. Damn.

My love. Oh, my love.

She was riven. She wanted so badly to pull Lex to his feet, to lose herself in those arms again, to feel that so-right embrace. But she couldn't do that. *No time.*

'Treem,' he croaked, his voice thick. Barely lucid. (And her choice was made.) 'Am I glad to see—'

Don't be, she thought, pulling him roughly off the strut because there was no time for anything more gentle. She twisted him over, reached for the emergency release, wished more than anything – almost anything – that it didn't have to end this way. But she'd *promised*.

And Cory was kin.

'Sorry, love,' she explained, sidestepping Lex's confused, urgent scrabbling as she lifted his air supply module free. 'Someone needs your air.'

lakeside

He had been following the dried course of a stream.

The streambed was a twisted ribbon that knotted its way around outcrops paled by past rainfall, through the canyon it had carved for itself – and would etch anew when the methane rains next returned – among the rough hillocks and peaks of crud-tarnished ice.

It was a rugged place, and, Åke felt, one which gave the lie to the complaint that Titan was an unrelenting brown wilderness. (Admittedly, the world was a study in monochromaticity; but there were, after all, *shades* of brown, and of orange, and even of yellow.) Seen from the air – and why wouldn't you, with Titan ideally shaped for flying? – the southern polar region was like nowhere else on the world.

The opportunity for sightseeing was welcome. Pity about his destination. He had nothing to say to Gerta.

From a couple of klicks up, it had been the transporter's grey rectilinearity, nothing more, that had marked it as incongruous against the dun polar landscape, competing for his attention with the dark oblong of Ontario Lacus starting ten kilometres or so towards the southern horizon. He had, at first, misinterpreted the vehicle's shape as a building, a new outpost; rare indeed in this region, in these difficult times. His curiosity sparked, Åke brought the Featherblade in lower, spiralling down through the soft brown pall of midsummer twilight.

At this altitude, he thought he could just discern the slow, broad waves – a series of gentle corrugations – that the prevailing wind would be patiently sculpting across the lake's dark liquid-ethane surface.

A childhood memory flared within him, unbidden. He'd been five, or maybe only four, and his father had taken him to a swimming pool. It must've been the public pool at Solà, a vast twenty-metre expanse of warmed water, in what seemed like the habitat's largest chamber. He'd been standing on the steps at the pool's shallow end, encased up to the neck flange by a small child's T-suit (which must have been a rental; he'd recalled being considerably older, ten or eleven, not long before that disastrous holiday, before he'd had a T-suit of his very own). His father, similarly suited, was standing hip-deep in the tepid pool, holding both Åke's helmet and his own. There was a sense of standoff – his father was almost as comfortable in a T-suit as in his own skin, while Åke himself was uneasy about something in the scenario, though at this remove he couldn't clearly work out whether that had been distrust of the liquid up to his own knees or some kind of claustrophobic resistance to the idea of pulling the helmet on.

He couldn't remember exactly how his father had tackled Åke's reluctance at the pool-test. But he did remember the immersion, the fear and then the wonder at the suit's ability to contain him safely against the water which enveloped him completely when he did, ultimately, step off into the deep end… and after that, it seemed like he'd pestered his father every break-day for the next six years, to take him exploring in the raw Titanian landscape which stretched around Solà.

Closer, and it became apparent there was something wrong in the vista below.

The transporter, a Mitsuda Longhaul from the look of it, lay upon its left side, nearly parallel to but not on the raised Via Australis trackway. The vehicle's cargo hatchway gaped open, dark. Two T-suited figures – no, three – were sprawled on the mucky ice around the Longhaul, motionless, their suits stained almost to camouflage by what had to be months, if not longer, of exposure to Titan's grimy precip. Which made, all up, for a puzzle: Via Australis was as sparsely travelled as any Titanian road, particularly since Atreya had cracked, but the transporter was close enough that it would certainly have been spotted by one of the first few mining, freight, or personnel-transport vehicles to have passed by. (He'd seen the white headlamps, blue tail-lights of a couple of small vehicles heading this way, just an hour or so ago.) For the crashed Longhaul to have lain undetected for anything beyond, at most, a day or two was scarcely conceivable.

It occurred to Åke only once he'd committed the nanothopter to its final semi-automated landing approach that there was an alternative explanation for the scene. An explanation which took better account of the wreck's still-glowing navlamps, of the lack of tholin-staining on the transporter's light-grey paneling, of the extensive damage now discernible to the vehicle's front tracks. The T-suited corpses had not been stained, by months of exposure, from their ubiquitous visibility-blue hue; rather, they had from the outset been coloured for camouflage. Which basically permitted two possibilities, both implying conflict, both presaging trouble.

What might have been carried by the transporter which could have drawn the attention, and it appeared the fire, of southern cantonment mil forces? How had they died? And if the figures of the dead weren't mil, but others for whom the donning of combat gear was dictated...

He should boost, he should push on to the arcology at Yelle, where Gerta would be expecting him. But the diorama of the transporter, and of its apparent ambushers, was static; the terrain was clear and devoid of obvious hazard. He had time, and Åke didn't feel any form of loyalty towards Gerta. Quite the reverse, in fact, for all that his mother, striving so hard to be even-handed (and was that through guilt, or remorse, or genuine affection?), pushed the relationship between him and his father's lover. *She's the last link you'll ever have to him*, Åke's mother had said; *he'd want the two of you to get along.*

Yet where in 'get along' did hatred fit?

*

Åke landed with an anticlimactic slow slide on the smoothest terrain he'd been able to spot, twenty metres or so on the eastern side of the fallen transporter. The road was a dark ridge that stretched straight, an artificial horizon ten to fifteen metres further west, behind the transporter; the bodies he'd seen from the air, strewn between road and vehicle, were currently eclipsed by the latter's blocky bulk. He felt safer for having landed out of sight of the carnage.

You don't have to be here, he reminded himself, pressing the controls to collapse the nanothopter. *You could be back up in the air right now, just a couple more hours to Yelle.* But he'd done a lot of time in the airframe today already. Some time spent exploring the wreck was still a confinement, of a sort (the sole attraction of Yelle, right now, and insufficient to overpower his enmity of Gerta, was that it would allow him to finally shuck the suit for a few days), but his legs would welcome the exercise. While he stretched, and sought to work out the kink that had caught at his neck, the 'thopter compacted itself down, folding itself into the suitcase-sized, squat-tripod-supported 'standby' mode that minimized heat loss to the chill environment. Machinery didn't function well at Titanian temperatures, and the standby geometry served to conserve battery power and thus maximize range. Moving the origami'd Featherblade close in to the lee of the fallen transporter's roof would keep it out of the slow but steady wind, and further reduce dissipation. He still had plenty of juice to reach Yelle, but there was no point in running a risk.

(So why was he here?)

This first one had died quickly. A slick-frozen, crimson-brown blot of blood had bloomed across the ground around the prostrated figure's T-suit, encroaching on and besmirching the long-barrelled firearm dropped by its side. Against Titan's crippling cold, a suited figure didn't leak much blood unless the wound, and therefore the puncture, was broad. So: a few seconds, not more. Åke fought the softly-scraping sensation of gorge rising in his throat. He'd seen death before, and death

93

unshielded by a T-suit's protective cocoon – anyone who'd assisted in the grim rescue effort at Atreya could scarcely have avoided it – but that had nonetheless been at a remove, through the grainy wraparound visuals of a remote recovery drone. This was immediate, purposeful, brutal.

A second, smaller assailant, sprawled on his (her?) back a half-dozen metres from the first, near the transporter's southward-pointing cab, would have perished even quicker. It took Åke just one hastily-averted glance to ascertain that it had been a head shot, the helmet's polymer visor crazed, scorched, and partially imploded on the left side. (Scorched? A flare-gun, then, perhaps?) He dared a second look. The blood-encrusted contents framed by the visor's mortal breach refused to resolve themselves into recognizable facial details. Bio-stat patches still glowed ruddily across the body's T-suited chest, confirming the obvious. A businesslike thick-barrelled weapon, with an oversized pistol-grip set somewhat behind its midpoint and a drum-shaped casing around its back end, had fallen a metre or so away from the woman. Was this what a personal missile platform looked like?

If that's really a PMP, Åke mused, *no wonder they went for the head shot.*

Steadying both his attention and his stomach, Åke moved forward around the wreck, to check out the Longhaul's cab. The vehicle's front was a mess, its windscreen shot in, two blue-suited figures slumped together, motionless, where they had fallen against the driver's-side airlock. Suited: so they'd been expecting trouble. Suits looked intact, though in all likelihood there'd be breaches from bullets or shrapnel.

Carefully skirting the dead woman and the missile launcher, he moved back along the muck-sprayed wall of the vehicle's tracked undercarriage to where the third assailant was propped, seated, splay-legged, against the front of the long median set of treads. This one had probably lasted longer, his posture speaking of some effort at minimising discomfort. The visor-enclosed face was contorted, frozen (by now, perhaps literally) in an anguished, angry grimace. The T-suit's casing had cooled sufficiently, since death, to allow the accumulation of a hydrocarbon frosting along its more wind-sheltered surfaces. The gloved fingers of the man's right hand still gripped his left forearm: futile effort to staunch a puncture? No blood, no more obvious damage to his camo-skinned suit: a small wound, then, not immediately fatal, and death most probably by Titan's patented combination of asphyxiation and blood-poisoning. (*Atreya*. Åke bit his lip, blinked hard, and forced himself to breathe evenly.) This man, too, had been armed. A rifle lay on the ground, a few metres further back, at the far end of the transporter's median treads.

He wouldn't have thrown the rifle, he'd have let it drop. So why was the rifle at the other end of the treads from the figure? There was no logical reason to move from one point to the other, except that at this point the latticework of the capsized transporter's underside made for a better climbing frame. Åke looked up. Four metres, max. And plenty of glove-holds.

It wasn't a difficult climb.

Viewed from above, the cargo hold was a mess. Åke wasn't game to climb down into the hold, for fear of difficulty in re-emerging. Nets designed to isolate flimsy cases of provisions from heavier, rather brutal looking items of machinery had failed to provide protection when the transporter had tipped. The Longhaul's climate-control system had evidently failed also. Some of the canned foodpacks (those that had not burst) were probably still secure, but the sight of so much Titan-spoiled produce (real vegetables and fruit, breached cartons of synthetic milk, a myriad fragments of shattered packaging) sparked disturbing memories.

In Atreya, just before they'd found his father, Åke had been piloting a troupe of semiautonomous rem-recs through the sector-three foodstore. The foodstore, three levels below the geochem lab suite which contained his father's office, had been in that wedge of the arcology which had subsided with catastrophic result when the unsuspected frozen-hydrocarbon substratum had asserted itself as a fracture plane in the settlement's ice foundations. A failure of the initial surveying, a fault of the hab's waste-heat engineering, a fundamental flaw in construction, a shortcoming in the arcology's crisis-management system: three years on, and the finger-pointing had not yet let up. It had been Titan's worst tragedy. Sixteen hundred dead, some quick like his father (anoxia), some agonizingly extended. Amongst those who had survived the atmospheric toxins' more immediate effects, the carcinogenicity was beginning to bite. (And Gerta? A clean bill of health…)

He shook himself back to the present. What amongst the transporter's cargo had been worth killing for? The foodstuffs? The unidentifiable machinery? That small, bulbous, vehicular-looking object in the gloom towards the rear? He doubted that any of it was particularly valuable: it was all, one way or another, carbon-based. Carbohydrate, protein, polymer, diamond. Nothing that looked like steel, no titanium, no iron ingots, nothing that counted as precious on a world where the very air snowed soot, and where even the most accessible mineral deposits were entombed below many kilometres of dirty ice.

And how had the attack happened? The ambushers presumably had been lying in wait, but they were dozens of kilometres from any settlement that Åke knew of. Even if, as seemed likely, they'd stationed themselves a few hundred metres back along the roadway, they still had to have some means of getting there. The Longhaul was the only vehicle here… he should check back along the road a way. Not too far, though; he should be getting airborne before too much longer, but these people wouldn't have walked in pursuit of the transporter if they'd needed to travel any particular distance. If they'd left vehicles, they shouldn't be far away.

Acting on a whim, he picked up the PMP.

The marks left by the transporter were clear enough, for backtracking purposes. The Longhaul had apparently tipped as soon as it had left the trackway. It had then skidded, uncontrolled, across the dirty ice, scraping off the ground's sepia-toned topcrust of organics as it went; the runoff-smoothed terrain, and the absence of any traction the treads would have afforded, had conspired to prolong its slide. But the ambush had occurred almost a hundred metres further north, back along the road, at the end of a long sloping right-hand curve as the Via Australis bent itself south towards the lake. The two skid-bikes – Hainan Icemasters, Åke noted, bywords in speed and raw power – were parked just off the road, in a natural dip which in winter's grip a decade or so hence would likely be one of many seasonal methane puddles and ponds; currently dry save for a boot-heel's depth of squelchy organic detritus, the pocket gully would have provided excellent ground-level concealment for the waiting attackers. Camouflaged as they were, and sufficiently far away from the crashed transporter, the Icemasters would very probably have eluded Åke's detection from the air, regardless… but unless he missed his guess, those incongruous-shaped dark canopies (which certainly did not seem to fulfil any identifiable aerodynamic purpose) must be stealth caps, designed specifically to evade aerial surveillance by radar or IR scanners. Mil stuff, proscribed from civilian use, jealously guarded.

And yet… the canopies had a rough and distinctly worn appearance to them, where from everything Åke had heard they were the kind of tech that took careful maintenance or lost function quickly. So, in all probability, *ex*-mil, which would fit also with the discarded rifle (plastic and diamond, home-printed, disposable in appearance) to be found on the ground between the two bikes. Plus, while the Icemasters did not display the kinds of alphanumeric ID markings that he would expect of mil vehicles, there was a prominent blue stencil-print of a splayed-finger handmark on the pannier casing of each bike. The handprints had a rude and inexpert look to them: likely they were gang marks, or (the suspicion firmed) pharmhands.

His gut tensed.

Pharmhands would not be convinced by explanations of innocence, of curiosity. Pharmhands would not be subject to any constraints of engagement. Didn't the ambush which must have played out here demonstrate that? Never mind all of the stories that got passed around, of pharmhand atrocities among the smaller habs and mining settlements.

Even if merely one-tenth of the apocrypha were true...

He really should get out of here. Gerta would be expecting him. There were worse things than staying with people you didn't care for, people you resented.

A shifting pattern of light caught at his eye. Headlights. There was a vehicle approaching around the bend, still some distance away. With a shock, he remembered the traffic he'd seen while still airborne. Two small vehicles, then; they'd looked most likely to be two-seaters. He could seek to hide, but if his suspicion was correct, any attempt at his concealment would be inadequate. Whoever was en route would very probably know the skid-bikes were here, and there simply weren't any other places to hide within easy reach. (Plus, blue T-suit, brown landscape, sore thumb...)

He could attempt to ambush *them*, to lie in wait with the PMP and blast them as they approached along the road. Judging by the damage sustained by the transporter's tracks and windshield, the missile-launcher would likely make mincemeat of a smaller vehicle. But Åke mistrusted the idea of bravery: he knew nothing of the weapon's operation, did not know even whether its atmosphere-shielded magazine still contained any rounds, and was insufficiently foolish to risk the danger of shrapnel, in an environment where any suit breach might as well be an unquenchable arterial wound. There was also the small matter that he didn't *know* the approaching vehicles to be hostile. For all he knew, they might be a family of miners, or a group of neo-Scientol missionaries. Unless or until, that is, they opened fire...

And if they *did* open fire... the pharmhands had apparently come by at least three major items of mil gear, as represented by the Icemasters and the PMP. It was a fair bet that this acquisition had not occurred in an entirely amicable and open-handed fashion. Pharmhands who could, by force, divest the mil of such equipment were not likely to be bested by a lone opponent wielding a weapon entirely unfamiliar to him.

He looked back towards the wreck of the transporter, thought about the time needed to run back, to unfold his nanothopter, to allow the Featherblade sufficient time to warm up that its rotors wouldn't simply shred or shatter as they attempted to rotate. Then he looked at the waiting skid-bikes.

It had been a long time since he'd ridden a skid-bike. (Why crawl, when you can fly?)

The idling Icemaster was noisier than he had expected, a persistent strong whine that resonated disconcertingly with his T-suit's neck-flange, and he couldn't find the controls to switch off its running lights. The bike's taillights would severely increase his visibility; and right now, that wasn't what he wanted. He climbed across the battery cowling, stirruped his boots as well as their spiked soles would allow, and canted the PMP so that the front of its magazine pressed against his suit's left hip, the barrel's business end balanced across the bike's handlebar. Holding the weapon in place with his left elbow was going to hamper his control of the Icemaster, but on the other hand to leave the PMP behind, with the other skid-bike, could be handing his notional pursuers a free shot. Flexing the bike's glove-grips, he gunned the batteries, increasing the pitch of the lightweight electric motors by the best part of an octave. The skids' traction belts sprayed up muck, and then bit into the packed ice beneath. He turned the front skid to climb over the lip onto the trackway.

The Icemaster, still cold, refused to accelerate as rapidly as he'd hoped, but it seemed to handle well enough. And he got fifteen seconds' advantage – not enough, not nearly enough – before the lighting from behind him changed from diffuse to direct, telling him that at least one of the vehicles behind had already cleared the bend. The bike's rear-view monitor wasn't steady enough to get a good look at the class of vehicle following him, and he was nowhere near game enough to turn around in his seat, but he suspected he was only four hundred metres ahead of it. He was, at least, still picking up speed.

Past the transporter, now. They must see it. Would they stop, when they drew level with it?

It seemed not. They were intent on pursuit.

The first gentle curve – on Titan, all bends were gradual – almost undid him, as he lost his grip on the PMP. It slid, tumbling from its awkward perch, hitting the road surface with sufficient speed that it bounced and spun off over the road's edge, onto the slope of the streambed. Åke barely managed to retain balance on the Icemaster. At least the bike would be easier to control now.

There were a lot of curves on this next stretch, where the road kept roughly parallel to the meandering course of the dry streambed as it made its way to Ontario's northeast shore. This suited Åke's purposes, for now: he was fairly sure that the bike was lighter and more manoeuvrable than whatever was following him. But the road would not keep bending—

A harsh *plak* interrupted his chain of thought, and the bike's power diminished markedly. A small round hole had suddenly appeared just below the top of the forward motor cowling. *I guess that answers the question of whether they're hostile*, he told himself. His gloves maintained their hold on the skid-bike's handlegrips, though his palms felt suddenly slick, his fingers weak and half-asleep.

He toggled the slider of the bike's master control one-handed, keeping his eyes firmly focused on the road. By switching all power to the rear-mounted motor, he could almost maintain his current speed, but at the loss of much of the Icemaster's road-handling. The road's bends were no longer a feature to his advantage. Plus, the battery indicator was showing an alarming rate of power drain. They'd have him, soon enough.

Having eased around the latest lazy corner, heart still racing, he chanced a look behind him. He thought he had maybe two minutes' lead on them now, not more. And then he'd reached lakeside – or rather, that stretch of the road which hugged the lake's winter high-liquid-mark. This far into summer, the shallow lake had receded several hundred metres back from the road.

It would get worse from here – fewer protective curves, fewer obscuring hills and headlands. If his pursuers were hoping for a clear shot at him, they wouldn't have long to wait.

Åke forced himself to think, to find some way to shake off his followers. If there'd only been time to get back to the 'thopter, to get himself airborne, to buy himself a whole extra dimension to play with...

But maybe there was.

There was a crossroads, or at least a K-intersection, a few kilometres ahead, just past the last substantial curve. The road led on past the lake, almost straight for many kilometres further; but there were two subsidiary roadways radiating off to the left, one heading northeast up the valley that led to Soderblom, the other east-southeast to Yelle. Both roads, at least initially, were far from straight, the valleys narrow and steep-sided. If he turned at that junction, it might not be immediately apparent which road he'd taken...

But they would see that he was no longer on the Via Australis, at any rate. So they'd know he'd taken either the Soderblom or the Yelle route, and they had two vehicles. The tactic would divide them, but it would not save him.

There were skeins of alkane fog ghosting across the road, drifting in the breeze. Ontario Lacus had crept in closer against the road, which here dropped away almost sheer for several metres at its edge, down to the lake's winter shoreline. The liquid's surface, ruffled by the wind into rows of low, lazy waves, was deep brown beneath the dark orange sky of late afternoon; haze robbed its further reaches of clarity. Now the hydrocarbon shore was just twenty metres from the trackway's edge; now fifteen; further ahead, before the curve that marked the road junction, the lake was virtually abutting the trackway's skirt, nuzzling at it. He struggled to review what he'd learnt of this region through geography, and through the frequent – and at the time, unappreciated – comments of his father, back when the three of them had still been a family, of sorts. Before Gerta, before those two, final, unreclaimable years.

The landscape around him brightened anew, and highlights and contrasting shadows spread and shifted along the bike's handlebars. He tensed, waiting for the impact at his back which would end all this (whether quick or slow), and willed the approaching curve closer.

The lake was five to fifteen metres deep along its eastern edge, he seemed to recall – his father had been full of such geographical detail. If the liquid continued to hug the road's edge after that curve, over that rise...

He bent into the curve, rode it out. Then he killed the Icemaster's engine and coasted to the trackway's shoreside lip before dismounting. Ahead lay the long straight that marked Ontario's northeast shore. Across from him, leading into the hills, the narrow routes to Soderblom and Yelle. He had a minute, maybe less. The bike was heavy, unwilling to shift, but with an anguished push he felt it tip forward, away from him, and then tumble ponderously into the lake. The splash was larger than expected, but with luck the ripples radiating outwards across the lake's hydrocarbon surface would be masked by the broader wave activity. He noted with satisfaction that the bike did not protrude above the surface at all. *Deep enough – good. Hopefully not too deep. Now comes the hard part.*

There weren't enough handholds, and the trackway's bank was almost sheer. The climb down was necessarily quick, but by no means graceful. He skidded down for most of the five metres, and arrested himself barely above the liquid's dark surface, perched on some unseen pouting of ice, clinging precariously to the tholin-crusted slope he was pressed against.

How terrified had he been, those fourteen years ago, at the edge of the pool at Solà? This much, or more?

He wished his father was here, now. But he must face these depths alone.

It occurred to him, belatedly, that Gerta hadn't entirely been the problem, that he'd allowed himself to be swayed by loyalty to his mother and her initial enmity to her replacement. The family had moved to Atreya before the breakup, before Gerta. It wasn't her fault she'd survived.

Gerta would be living with her memories of Åke's father, same as he was. Different memories, of course, but still...

A part of him once again four years old, he relinquished his grip, pushed down, and allowed himself to slide into the lake's chilled, fizzing, enveloping depths.

The light from above the surface brightened, flared, then ebbed. He waited, ignoring the lake's hyper-cold grasp on the suit's limbs, the spreading patches of frosted condensation on the visor's inner surface, until he judged that the last traces of vehicle-light had gone; then, digging his gloved fingers into the lake-bank's mucky detritus, he pulled himself stiffly up out of the liquid's embrace and clambered back up to the now-deserted trackway. The chill of his brief immersion still clung to him.

Idiots, he thought. *Sometimes it pays to look beneath the surface.*

It'd be about a ten kilometre walk back to the Longhaul, to retrieve the nanothopter. Call it two hours, though he hoped he could cover it more quickly than that. Another hour further, and he could be at Gerta's, trying to work out where he stood on the thorny issue of allegiance…

He was surprised to note that he was looking forward to describing his escape to her. It would be something to tell, and something more, too. A laurel branch, or whatever they called it. Or at least an icebreaker.

He hoped the 'thopter would still be there, concealed, back by the wreck of the transporter.

erebor

Guerline tires of the banter between her brother Freyne and Kim N'Diaye, who are arguing – skiting, really – over whether Erebor truly deserves to be called a mountain compared to the likes of Doom or the Mithrims which, of course, they've both also scaled. *Typical*, she thinks. *It's not about the experience, not about the views; it's about showing off. Men are so shallow.* She pauses, takes a long drink of water from her suit's refreshment nipple. Her suit is old, its systems struggling: the water carries a faint aftertaste of lunch's soup from two hours ago.

The climb has been comparatively steep, starting from a sharp gully that cuts deep into the western flank of Erebor's broad, irregular cone. It is, Guerline admits to herself, worth it for the views. Westward, backlit by the Sun still low enough in the early-morning sky that Erebor's intrinsically squat shadow still stretches for many kilometres, the dark longitudinal dunes extend towards the horizon's ochre haze like the furrows carved by some gigantic plough – or like the smudgy ridges of a yet more enormous fingerprint. North and east, the cryovolcano's slopes descend haphazardly towards the weathered stained-ice massif of Quivira, its edges steaming as the slow-rising sun burns off the long night's ethylene frosting. To the south, the view is impeded by the summit, silhouetted against a bleary-brown ominous sky, for they have not climbed to the peak, but to a high shoulder some hundred metres beneath the highest point.

Freyne is all for completing the climb, but Lon – alongside Guerline, the group's other novice – is adamant that, after the undulating six kilometres cross-country from their vehicle, and then the ascent of the western flank, they've done enough exertion for one morning. Though the rise to the summit is classed as an easy climb, it would mean several kilometres' trek across the mountain's upper reaches. Guerline is inclined to throw her vote in with Lon, and when Kim echoes those thoughts, it is only Neve, busy reconstructing a cairn out of several amber-coloured, wind-smoothed boulders of ice while the others bicker and plan, who truly sounds disappointed; even her own brother, Guerline thinks, has made the suggestion to persevere only for form's sake rather than out of any particular desire to go further. It is, after all, hardly a real mountain, and therefore not worthy of any serious effort. But perhaps it's unfair of her to impugn his motives so.

They walk a short distance along the ridge and find a slight hollow within which they can shelter from the worst of the persistent, growly wind that pushes its way across the mountaintop. They sit, drink their snacks in the curious communal isolation that is an out-of-doors mealtime gathering: an archipelago of T-suits. Guerline is reminded, as it seems she is on every infrequent sortie into the Titan wilds, that she should get around to replacing her own suit, which she has had since her days as an undergraduate and which was by no means new when she acquired it. Sitting, she can feel the cold of the volcano's deep-frozen ice seep with depressing efficiency through the inadequate insulation of the suit's seat: the sensation is not severe enough to be much more than an irritation, but a similar effect evidently gets too much for the equally ancient-suited Lon, who soon stands. And wanders off to attend, perhaps, to nature's call in something approximating privacy.

Neve makes a joke about life in Trafton; Guerline's heard it before, but evidently Freyne hasn't, because he laughs politely. Guerline inspects as much as she can make out of her brother's face through his helmet's translucent, half-chromed visor – she knows her friend likes him, worships him, almost, though shy Neve has never conceded as much to him – but he's not giving anything away, doesn't make eye contact. Guerline feels a dull sense of disappointment on Neve's behalf.

The conversation putters along, loftball and local amenities policies, and it's some minutes more before it occurs to Guerline that their wanderer hasn't returned.

'Where's Lon?' she asks, louder than is perhaps merited.

'I think he went to fill his tank,' Kim ventures.

'Yes, but that was ten minutes ag—'

There's a yell: loud, quick, unnaturally arrested. Guerline lurches to her feet, stumbles while pulling herself out of the hollow because the servoes along her suit's right leg have half-seized through inactivity and cold. She lands awkwardly, her glove's palm – sluggish servoes, again – not yet ready to arrest her momentum. A sharp pain lances through her wrist. *Sprained*, she tells herself, biting back an expletive. *Or worse. Shit.* She uses her other hand to push herself up, commands her suit to lock her sleeve to hold the wrist immobile.

The others rouse themselves in a rustling, raspy flurry. Kim looks confused; Neve anxious; Freyne has switched to take-charge mode. 'Stay here,' he instructs Guerline, pointing to the hollow, on learning of her wrist; the subtext being, she presumes, that an injured limb makes her a liability rather than an asset on a rescue mission. (She's not inclined to disagree, but it seems a callous assessment nonetheless.)

There's no sign of Lon; no sound, either. Erebor's heights are expansive enough that, in Kim's earlier words, 'it would take a special talent to fall from slopes that, for the most part, you can bike up', but, to set against that, Guerline's classmate has vanished. She feels her pulse quickening. The others troop off along a rough path to the east. She sees their bobbing heads, hears their strained-breath anxious chatter for a couple of minutes, but then they've passed beyond the range of her aging suit's receiver. She's alone, on a mountaintop, with an injured wrist. She tries not to think how this could end.

*

She has her suit read to her for a spell, from its onboard library. But she's not in the mood to invest in Susan Calvin's calm, clinical problem-solving, and soon she instructs it to stop. She stands, peering fruitlessly along the paths leading roughly east from the hollow.

It's growing uncomfortably hot in the suit. There's an intermittent fault with the thermostat, which tends to drift when she's been out in the suit for a few hours at a stretch; they've looked for the fault the last couple of times she's put the suit in for its annual service, but the problem with intermittent faults is, well, the intermittency... They replaced the thermostat last time, but that evidently hasn't fixed it. It tends to come right after a few minutes, and in the meantime she blinks away sweat, takes a long sip of water. At least the suit's water reservoir is still cold.

She wonders, idly, how many people die on Titan every year from overheating T-suits. Or, perhaps, from removing their helmet so as to 'just cool down a little'.

What can be keeping them?

Should she go after them? But she's not even completely sure, anymore, which of the ridge's hesitantly-defined paths they took, and an inaccurate guess could prove catastrophic. *But I can't just stand here waiting for my air to turn bad.* She decides, instead, to climb back down to the vehicle. Solo. With a sprained-or-broken wrist. In a suit that occasionally blooms with internal heat.

Guerline, is this wise?

Yes. Yes, it is. If they catch up on the way back, there's no harm done. If I still haven't sighted them, I can call in med assistance from the crawler.

But if they don't realise I've climbed back to it...

She needs to leave a note. She pats her thigh pouches, strives to remember which one contains the recorder. Recollects that she'd left the recorder on the crawler seat. *Damn.*

She crouches, leans forward; kneeling would feel more natural, but she'd have to use her sore wrist for balance. She's attempting the task of carving with her gloved finger some sort of rudimentary message – just a crudely-scribed arrow, she hasn't the patience for anything more elaborate –

in the largest uninterrupted patch of crusted tholin that she can find in the hollow's immediate vicinity. She can see the arrow in her mind, clean ice showing through the brown-black deposit of atmospheric crud, but the thin layer of tholin isn't well-anchored to the rock-hard ice beneath it, and it first shifts beneath the force of her glove, then, as she pushes more firmly, crumbles into a mosaic of messy, glove-staining flakes. It's not going to work; she's going to need to try something else. She stands, carefully, slowly: her calves ache from the squat, so do the balls of her feet. She's taking another sip of water, and staring at Neve's cairn wondering whether there are enough boulders in it to fashion an unambiguous arrow sign, when she becomes aware of a vague noise, not her, not the mountain, not the wind.

She turns: there's a suited figure approaching.

One suit. Not four. Red roundel: Freyne. 'What—' she gets out, before she can place the noise as the rasp of her brother's laboured breath. Her brother, who complained that Erebor wasn't a real mountain. It strikes her that if Freyne, whose ascent of the cryovolcano earlier this morning had seemed near-effortless, is winded, then something bad has happened. 'Is Lon alright?' she asks, stricken with anxiety as he draws near, fruitlessly striving to meet his visor-obscured eyes.

'He's alive,' he replies, his voice buzzing in her earpieces, and then he's fully occupied for several seconds with, it seems the task of breathing. 'He fell, over a hundred metres. Kim and Neve are still trying to find a way to winch him up safely. They sent me back to collect ropes and harnesses from the crawler.'

'Is he alright?'

'He's broken something, probably his tibia. And his transmitter's out. He's not having the best time of it. But I'd best keep moving. See you on the way back through.'

'Freyne,' she says, 'I'm not doing anything useful here. I may as well make the descent with you.'

His stance shifts. He appraises her – she knows the look, even through all the distorting optics of peering into another's visor. She sees the calculation in his gaze. Perhaps it's just something climbers do in this situation; but it seems redolent of arrogance and dismissiveness, and she doesn't like it.

'But your wrist,' he explains, his voice now back to its normal resonance. He's got his breath back. 'I'm not planning on using the ramp.'

'Ramp?'

'The route we came up.'

Lowering herself over the rim has to be the hardest thing, Guerline thinks, that she's ever done. *And Freyne was looking at doing this alone?* She has hold of the rope, which in any case is secured to her suit via a harness, and the rope is also harnessed to her brother as well as anchored, in some manner she's still not completely sure of, to the rock-solid ice a couple of metres back from the lip. But there's no denying – as her centre of gravity shifts ever closer to, and then over, the dubious security of the rim – that she's well out of her comfort zone. She's spectacularly bad with heights, and it's all she can do, dangling there one-handed while trying desperately, through the bulky, insensitive soles of her T-boots, to feel for the thick C-fibre rung that Freyne assures her is somewhere just beneath her...

'Got it,' she announces, breathless with the relief of it. As though this first rung is the only one that's necessary, the only one that matters. There's a few seconds' static.

'You got it?' he asks, as his helmet peers down at her like a gargoyle. He can't have heard.

So is my transmitter playing up, on top of everything else? 'Yes, I've got it.'

'You're tethered to the rung?'

'What? No, I can't reach.'

'What do you mean you can't reach?'

'If I bend down to clip the rope to the rung,' she explains, 'I'll lose my balance.'

'The rungs are at a half-a-metre spacing. You need to climb down to the second rung, then you can clip the end to the top rung.'

'There's no need to shout.'

'Climb down a step. There's enough play in the rope.'

There isn't enough play in the rope.

There's the top rung at, she thinks, about mid-shin height; she only has Freyne's word that there's another rung beneath that, anywhere down this cliff-face. She could look down, but she can't; she just can't. Her feet aren't resting on anything; she can feel the dread emptiness of the air behind her trying to suck her off the cliff.

'Stuck,' she reports. holding onto the rope for all she's worth, though tactile transmission through the small servoes on her nonspecialised gloves' thick fingers is almost nothing. A horrible thought occurs: what if she grips the rope so tightly that her gloves' servoes sever it? She's never heard of such a thing happening, but it would be just her luck. She sees herself – in her mind's eye, in her overworked imagination – fall limitlessly down the rust-stained beige-ice cliff, scraping and bouncing against protrusions, impacting at the base; she closes her eyes, slackens her one-handed grip. Suspended. Just waiting for disaster.

'Give me a minute. I'll shift a tether up here.' Her brother is so businesslike, so untouched by her terror, that she could scream.

She doesn't, of course. But her voice is croaky. 'Wait!' she calls, too loud. The suit is back to a comfortable ambient, but she doesn't like to think about how much sweat is still pouring off her. 'I should be able to reach the next rung from here.' She stretches her arm down, twists a little, bending against the suit's stiffened confinement, does indeed manage, just, to make glove contact – she thinks – with the uppermost rung. But then it takes her a minute, hampered by her dire need to avoid accidentally loosing the rope from her harness, until she's located the carabiner at the free end of the rope. It takes a further two minutes of blind fumbling with thickly gloved fingers until she's satisfied that she's clipped the carabiner down to the rung that's barely within reach. 'All good. I think.' Breathless.

'Slide down until you can grip the top rung,' he advises. She does so, latches on grimly. It seems only a few seconds and then Freyne, who has miraculously found something on which to grip on his traversal down the top two metres of what she recollects to be sheer, stained but otherwise featureless smooth ice, is standing on the same rung as her; and then he has climbed down past her. After a short interval she feels a tug, a thrum, on the rope. 'I'm clipped here. Unclip. And climb down,' he advises.

At least his voice has dropped below a shout.

'Frey,' she says, 'I *can't*. My wrist.'

'Guer, you have to.'

'For all I know, my wrist could be broken.'

'It's not broken – I've interrogated your suit's med-stats. And even if it were, there's enough strength and dexterity in your suitsleeve's servoes to manage basic power-grip functions like that. You'll still need to use your good hand for the clipping and unclipping, but your glove can hold a rung.'

She tries it. Pain slashes through her right wrist, but if she angles her forearm so she's not fighting against the suit's splint-lock, it's manageable. She reaches down with her left hand, finds the rung her end of the rope is clipped to, gingerly lowers herself until she feels – always at a further distance than she expects – her boot-tips on the next rung down. She brings her right hand down – more pain – to hold the rung while she unclips the rope's carabiner from the rung. Her legs won't stop shaking.

Climb. Down.

It's a ten-metre rope; the rungs are fifty centimetres apart. She can descend, in one sequence, about thirty rungs, passing Freyne at the midpoint. She doesn't think she'll ever complete the task, but she does. Fifteen metres closer to *terra firma*.

The respites, while Freyne does his share of the descent, are dispiritingly brief. She's ashamed at how dramatically she is delaying him.

But if her brother is impatient with the rate at which she's descending the cliff-face, he doesn't show it. Instead, so as to distract her from her panic, he tells her how the rope is resistively warmed to a temperature of minus fifty, a hundred and thirty degrees above Titan ambient, for pliancy; how the rungs are anchored into the only cliff-face on Erebor's western slopes, and had been put in for maintenance access for a planned tourist funicular/elevator which has never been built, whether for reasons of financial viability or of sustained opposition from Titan recreationalists, Freyne is not certain; how the youngest person to have abseiled the cryovolcano is—

He slips, several rungs above Guerline, as he's descending. He yells something she can't make out. For several disbelieving heartbeats she watches him fall, with seemingly choreographed fluidity, towards her, and then, with a bruising thump, more rapidly past her. She holds on. She's gripping her rung with both hands, while the rope seems to pull in two directions at once. It's a ten-metre rope: Freyne falls perhaps seven metres past her before Guerline, still dazed from the knock, suddenly and sharply becomes the primary anchorage point. There's a jolt that flows like lightning through the harness, through her shoulders, through her arms. Her gloved holds on the rung are torn loose; and she falls too, twisting as she's pulled after her brother. It's the twist which saves her, since when, with a sharp both-ways tug against gravity, the still-fastened carabiner above yanks her (and some distance below her, Freyne) to a painfully sudden halt, it's the suit's solidly-reinforced backtank casing which knocks sharply against the unyielding rung-studded cliff-face, and not the strengthened but substantially more brittle curve of her visor. The adrenaline kicks in, and she's hanging there, swaying against the cliff, panting with dread and facing outwards. Hydrocarbon mist and still-shaded beige ice, much too far below. She's covered in cold sweat. Her heart is racing like an overwound clockwork.

She was wrong to think her wrist hurt before. This is much worse. And an impact to her left-hand glove, against a rung or some irregularity in the cliff's ice face, has set that hand – her good hand – afire with pins and needles.

She still has air, she can't hear or smell a leak anywhere. And pissing yourself in a suit designed to unremarkably process such eventualities isn't, she supposes, anything to feel ashamed about. But something in her has decided this is all too much, and she's in shock. She cannot find it in herself to move.

Belatedly, she wonders about Freyne, beneath her, who has fallen much further and therefore might well have sustained substantially worse damage than has she. She envisages his breached helmet, a ruptured air-line, even a crushed heating panel; he has, she knows, an adventurer-grade T-suit, ruggedised against all manner of hazards, but Titan has so many ways to kill. By cold, by asphyxiation, by toxicity and even, it would seem, by gravity…

He climbs up to her. When he reaches the rung beneath her she can hear that he is calling out to her, asking if she's OK. His radio isn't working, or maybe it's hers. She suspects he's shouting again, but it's all rather indistinct: the suits muffle the noise. What works best, it turns out, for sound transmission is for Freyne to rest the side of his helmet against her abdomen, just below her med-status panel: it's an oddly intimate pose.

'Can you climb down?'

She shifts her left arm past his helmet so she can grip the rung at chest height, but her glove's fingers won't close on the anchored C-fibre rod. The control system for the servoes, sheathing the back of her hand, must have been damaged by the impact. *Sans* servo action, the glove should still be sufficiently flexible for basic manipulation… but it's an old suit. Her hand might as well be gloved in wood. 'No. I'm sorry, Frey, but I can't. The glove's dead.'

'Then I'll lower you. You'll have to clip your carabiner to the lowest rung you can reach, but I can do the rest. Can you manage that?'

'I don't know. I have to, don't I? But the radio – how will you know whether I've fastened it?'

'Hand signals. You ready?'

'Sooner we start, the sooner we finish.'

'That's about it. OK, I'm clipped on. Unclipping your end now. Right, I've got the slack. Lowering now.'

It's jerky, and she knows she should be terrified, but what she feels right now is mostly exhaustion. She drops down, tentative, erratic, like a baited hook, and when after several metres the descent stops, she reaches – pain – for the carabiner and fumbles – pain – with it until she gets it fastened to the rung at her midriff. Then she reaches up and flashes a thumbs-up. Pain.

He climbs down to her level, clips himself, unclips her. Commences to lower her anew. *Wash. Rinse. Dry. Repeat.* And so it goes.

She's all for moving on, without further delay, to get back to the crawler, but after the steep and treacherous scree slope that overpowers the last twenty metres of the rungway, Freyne insists on a short rest stop. Which isn't really a rest stop, because he uses the time to damage-assess their suits and gear following the rigours of the chaotic descent. She's astounded that it's taken them less than an hour to reach the mountain's base – in her subjective assessment, she would have said three.

She wonders, guiltily, how quickly he might have managed it if unencumbered by a novice.

She's sitting on a shelf of outcropped ice thick with a coating of flaky tholin, but it's not as if her T-suit wasn't stained before. She's glad of the respite, notwithstanding her mild protestations – she needs the opportunity to persuade her heart that *it's all right now, it's over;* except, of course, that they still need to get the equipment required to rescue Lon. But Freyne reckons they can take the crawler around Erebor's base and reach his location from below, which just leaves Kim and Neve to make the descent themselves. All in all, it seems the best approach.

While she's perched on the outcropping, her suit's inadequate insulation ensures that her backside is soon chilled. When it starts tingling, she takes it as a sign that it's time to stand, which her brother takes as a sign that it's time to push on. He's never been inclined to linger. They push on. Fifteen to twenty minutes later, she's almost steaming in her suit: the thermostat-fault, again. *The personal sauna experience,* she tells herself. The uncomfortable heat makes it difficult to concentrate on negotiating the terrain, and she thinks of asking Freyne to wait with her until the suit settles back to a more acceptable equilibrium. But there's the urgency of Lon's rescue; she perseveres. The heat ebbs. And she makes a connection.

It happens, each time, awhile after I've sat down, she thinks. *It must be some kind of delayed overreaction to the insulation's failure.* She smiles to herself: it's a small victory, to set against the defeats Titan has lined up for her today, but it does indeed feel like a triumph of a sort, against Titan, against her suit, against the blind impersonal forces that can kill you. She's puzzled it out. Susan Calvin would be proud.

It takes long enough to walk back to the crawler that she starts to feel light-headed, so she takes a few long sips of grainy, lukewarm broth. And wonders if the newer suits offer better cuisine...

She rounds an obstacle, behind Freyne, and the crawler at last slips into view.

'Sit down, strap yourself in,' he advises through the crawler's comms system, as, seated in the control cage, he switches on the vehicle's big whiny electric motors.

Guerline eyes the Titan-cold passenger bench, opts instead to grip the roll-cage support beside it, planting her feet to compensate, as best as possible, for the crawler's motion across the uneven terrain. 'No, I'd just rather stand,' she explains.

It marks the only expedition on which Guerline accompanies her brother. She can see the attractions that climbing holds, she's aware Freyne values such things, she admires him for it. It is, after all, an important part of who he is. But it's not for her.

All of which means, of course, that she's not with him, and Neve, and Kim N'Diaye, on that tragic expedition some half-dozen years later, from which Freyne doesn't return. She's half the world away, safe, suddenly bereft in her helplessness. For some months afterwards she hates both Kim and Neve for surviving, for carrying on, just as she hates herself for not being there. Such feelings don't benefit anyone, though, and after a time she lets them ebb.

But the way ahead is always difficult, and some days she cannot find the next rung.

goldilock

'Hold still,' warned the pharmhand, voice tinny through Cory's earbud.

Cory, lying visor-down – his face, aflame, insulated from the sepulchral gritty-ice landscape by two layers of semismart polymer – redoubled his futile efforts to throw his assailant off. What was the bastard doing to the back of his suit?

'Hold *still*, damn you, Cory!'

Perhaps not a pharmhand. Cory, his suit's air now fully bad, held still. 'Lex?' he asked, almost inaudibly.

No response. No movement at all, for several seconds. Cory was sinking into what might well have been that final, troubled drift when the squatter, heavy on his back, rushed into a paroxysm of activity, thumping at something that sat where Cory's backtank should have been, jolting this thing from the right, then the left. 'Close your mouth,' the voice advised, giving the lump on the back of Cory's suit an almighty wallop. There was an appalling stink of Titan – old death, stale piss, burnt metal – and behind it, plentiful, cold, clean, breathable air. Cory passed out.

'Cory, you need to chill.' And now he did recognise those contralto tones.

'Teresa?' he asked. Retched. Took a sip of tholin-flavoured water; spat it out, directing it well away from the visor. Took another sip: better, but still blood-hot. Tried again. 'Teresa Maria?'

'You need to spill heat,' she told him. *So much for pleasantries*. But she was right. He was feverish.

She'd pulled his suit into a sitting position, had him propped up against something – the flyer? – and was holding his right arm horizontal, awkwardly. The arm hurt; other parts hurt more. The nightsuit's scaffolding cut into bruises on legs and torso. Plus, thanks to the suit's scroogish shepherding of heat, his whole body was cooking in its own cascading sweat.

Still, one word would remedy the latter. He screwed his eyes shut. 'Flash,' he directed, bracing himself for a redistribution of pain.

Nothing happened.

'*Flash*,' he repeated, eyes again closed. *Marinating in my own juices here, Suit...*

'Cory,' said Teresa Maria, her grip on his sleeve slipping. 'You're still on Comms. Activate Ops.'

'Alt ops effect flash,' he declared, lifting his arm a fraction; then realised, too late, that he'd forgotten to close his eyes. His own personal lightning bolt – technically, an afterglow marking the path of the UV-A photon pulse emitted from the cooling laser housed in his nightsuit's sleeve – scribed a brilliant pencil-beam across the ice-strewn, night-cloaked valley, sunbursting against an outcrop two hundred metres distant. His visor overloaded, flickering off then on.

The laser's awful dizzying cold bit into the skin, then the muscle and bone of his right arm, and he passed out again.

'Dayani?' he asked Teresa Maria. He hadn't been out long. Arm still a frozen stump, slowly thawing; the rest of him still hot. Need to take another shot soon: thermal camo's double-bind.

Before answering, Teresa Maria fired down a pulse herself, directing the beam aft. 'Never stood a chance,' she said, rawness transcending the earbud's minimal sonics. 'Cory, the two of us will be damn lucky to escape with our lives. Forget the CREV's cargo. No amount of metal is worth this.'

'Lex?'

Facial expression couldn't be read through a nightsuit. The suits' sumoid bulk also swamped finer nuances of gesture, but there was no mistaking the pain in Cory's aunt's eventual response. 'Lex is dead, hon. I found him just round there, on the flyer's other side, and I – I couldn't save him. They'd holed his suit above the knee.'

'Oh.'

'That's his air supply on your back. They'd wrecked yours.'

'Aunt Teresa, I'm so sorry.'

'Not your fault,' she replied.

'I mean, I know Lex meant a lot to you.' He could feel himself colouring up; talking about emotional subjects with the older generation was always awkward. But the anonymifying nightsuit provided flawless camouflage.

'Cory,' said Teresa Maria, '*you* mean a lot to me. There'll be time to grieve later. I hope. We need to get away. This flyer isn't airworthy anymore. Walking's not an option, not with Ponnamperuna seventy klicks away. The dirigible would cut us down in no time. And there are still at least four pharmhands back at the CREV – they could be here in minutes. There's no chance your cooling blast escaped their attention.'

'I'm sorry,' he said.

'Done now. They knew we were here anyway, so it doesn't change anything.'

'Except they know we're *still* here,' said Cory. 'Look away.' He sighted on a fallen figure – the pharmhand, he thought, that had tried to kill him, now himself lying lifeless on the deep-frozen valley floor twenty-five metres away, cooling towards ambient. Target acquired, his suit informed him, and, his right arm outstretched like a falconer, his eyes squeezed tightly shut, he gave the laser its head. The arm-chill this time was less severe: no inclination to black out, but he did feel a twinge of nausea...

The pharmhand's T-suit showed a localised bright patch in IR, on its abdomen, where the laser pulse had struck it. It was an uncomfortable thing, Cory decided, to fire at a human target, even a dead human target, but he could do it if he had to. These people had tried to kill him. *Would* have killed him, but for Teresa Maria's intervention… and Lex's death. There was no comfort in that last thought either. Guilt? Plenty. He patted his thigh-pouch for reassurance, fumbled out a small flat envirosealed package, gazed at it a few seconds and then secreted it away again.

Body language, in a nightsuit, was muted, but something about his aunt's unmoving stance was challenging. 'What?' he asked.

'And that little show-and-tell was…?' There was a warning in Teresa Maria's voice, something he very much didn't understand.

'Arum,' Cory explained carefully. 'I had some pix of her with me. I just needed to see that they hadn't been damaged in the fight.'

'Jesus, Cory, what is *wrong* with your priorities? You really think we've got time for you to be daydreaming about your lover?'

'I was – Aunt Teresa, I'm sorry. But I wasn't daydreaming. I was just taking a moment to collect my thoughts.'

'I still think it shows…' But Teresa Maria did not expand upon what she thought it showed.

'So does Arum *know* about this?' she asked, stretching her arms to encompass the wrecked flyer, the desolate Titanian nightscape, the as-yet-unseen approaching pharmhand reinforcements. 'Don't get me wrong, I like your Goldilocks, she seems good for you, but—'

'Goldilocks?'

'Isn't that your pet name for Arum?' Teresa Maria asked. 'I heard you tell Dayani—'

'No, that was something different,' said Cory. 'And no, Arum doesn't know. I mean, she wouldn't approve, she knows I've hacked, but only small stuff. I wouldn't dream of telling her about the CREVjacking, she'd throw her tank.'

'It's still weird how they got the drop on us,' said Teresa Maria. 'We hadn't even reached the CREV; and how long does it take to prep a dirigible? They knew we were coming.'

'Could've been blind luck. Training flight.'

'Doubt it. But we're wasting time. Those four at the CREV will turn up eventually.'

'Not just those four. There are more on the way,' he told her.

'You know this how?'

'When we – when Lex and I got back to the flyer, before they dropped from the dirigible, I had a couple of minutes to monitor for comms. I overheard some traffic between the dirigible and a ground vehicle. It mentioned a couple of quad-skis, and more personnel. They were maybe ninety minutes away at that point.'

'Less than half that now, then. Any idea how many personnel?'

'Things got kinda busy here,' said Cory.

'Something doesn't tally,' Teresa Maria reported, having returned with several weapons. 'The pharmhands I checked were both decked out in mil-quality T-suits – camo, armoured, visors about the only vulnerable feature – but their guns are third-rate. Look.' She presented a weapon to Cory.

'At what?' he asked, giving it a once-over then handing it back.

'Home-printed,' she said, struggling with glove-pudgy fingers at the housing of the gun's top-loading magazine. 'And this ammunition isn't armour-piercing,' she explained, spilling three bullets into her palm. The bullets were polymer: on hydrocarbon- and ice-dominated Titan, metal bullets – in fact metal anything – would be prohibitively expensive. (Hence the lure of an entire cargo of offworld ore had been irresistible. *Almost* irresistible.) 'Dum-dums, not even self-powered.'

'So?'

'In this atmosphere, they're strictly short-range weapons. I mean, this is just one step up from a disposable. I tried firing one of these before, and it seized on me. They're not well made. This ammo wouldn't work well against their suits – too soft, just spreads out on impact. Be lethal against a regular T-suit, close enough range, though – nice big breach, quick asphyxiation even if the wound itself isn't too severe. Against our suits? Somewhere in between – there's a lot of padding with the insulation, so the chance of an actual breach, or of major damage to internal organs isn't so bad. But damage to the heat-reg system is a risk, ditto the laser optics. And we're always vulnerable to a head shot.'

'They got Lex in the leg, you said.'

'Lucky shot,' Teresa Maria replied, surveying the horizon.

'And you said Dayani was killed instantly,' Cory protested.

There was something cold in his aunt's voice when she answered, as if she was accusing him of – what? 'Whatever's in the dirigible, which is where they gunned down Dayani from, must use self-powered ammo, possibly even micromissiles. Clearly, that's not what the footsoldiers get.'

'Why does this matter?'

'It limits our options, Cory. A quad-ski's not a brilliant escape vehicle, but it beats walking. Trouble is, we'll have to fight for it. We can't get much mileage from these weapons; and we don't know, yet, how many more pharmhands we'll face, nor whether they'll be better armed, nor how much they know about our nightsuits. We could retain a tiny whisker of advantage, or we could be supremely vulnerable. We won't know until they show. Best case, they'll be using night vision, so we'll be invisible in the suits. Worst case, they'll have searchlights and PMPs. We just don't know.'

'So we wait here, by the flyer?'

'No. Flyer's too obvious. We wait somewhere else. *Lex* waits here.'

'But Lex is – oh. You mean as a decoy?'

'Cory, dead is dead. We can't afford sentiment.'

'Guess not, but – where will we be?'

She pointed across to a long, low, barrow-like rise that started about a hundred metres away. 'Difficult not knowing for sure which way they'll approach from. But the dirigible came from the east. So the ridge seems as good as anything, in terms of cover. I'll wait there.'

'You? What about me?'

'Cory, we're talking gunfight. I need you to stay safe. We rig up the night-tarp, they won't even—'

'So you don't trust me, is that it?' he asked, surprising himself at the hurt in his voice. 'This is the CREV all over again.'

'Cory, *no*, I'd trust you with my life,' she replied, and after a few seconds, quieter, 'I just don't trust myself with yours.' She looked up, scanned the terrain. 'I made a promise to your mother—'

'Aunt Teresa,' said Cory, 'I can fight my own battles.'

The suits were cumbersome. It was not far to the rise which Teresa Maria had identified as a defensive rampart, but it took several minutes: while rapid movement in the nightsuits was possible *in extremis*, it came at a cost.

'Damn.'

'What?' Cory asked.

'I just realised – if we get separated, I'll have no way of reliably seeing where you are, unless the visor's on visual. And then the pharmhands will be camo'd. So I can keep track of you or the pharmhands, but not both. That's not good, in a combat situation.'

'You're not using fullview?'

'Fullview?'

'It's an overlay I did for the visors,' Cory explained. 'It upshifts IR and compresses vis so it's all visible at once. Takes a bit of getting used to – you need to remember that reds and oranges are IR, blues and greens are vis, and it's laggy by a half-second – but it should help. I'm sure I mentioned it during the flight.'

'Guess I was preoccupied.'

'I think we all were. Aunt Teresa, what if they don't show?'

'What d'you mean?'

'We're assuming the pharmhands will be back. But they might decide to take the CREV's cargo and not bother about us – which case, we're stuck.'

'Cory, we're witnesses. They don't leave witnesses. They'll show. One way or another, we won't have to worry about walking home.'

It went from there.

The quad-ski presented fewer problems than they'd anticipated, once they'd disabled the vehicle's searchlight. Thermal camouflage was an enviable battlefield advantage, in the Titan night. Four against two; then three against two; then two against two; then one against two. Teresa Maria had seen to securing the quad-ski, while Cory mopped up.

The last pharmhand's gun had seized; Cory's hastily-targeted laser pulse had deflected off his opponent's armoured helmet, scorching it but not inflicting a lethal blow, and he wasn't warm enough to pulse again. But Cory still had a gun tethered at his hip, and he aimed this now. The pharmhand raised his (her?) arms in surrender, and Cory found he lacked the impulse to determine whether his gun would, in fact, fire.

He stared at the pharmhand for a good half-minute, running through the options. Presumably there would be rope or cable in the quad-ski's cargo hatch, but he'd need Teresa Maria's cooperation for that. And then there would be the prob—

There was a burst of sharp blue-white, a neat instantaneous circle at the centre of the pharmhand's visor, which quickly bloomed into a small, glowing, involuting flower on the helmet's faceplate. The flower spread its petals, withered, and cooled, leaving a ragged opening through which Titan's ultra-cold and unforgiving atmosphere was already rushing in. Cory could not, mercifully, discern the extent to which the pharmhand's face had been savaged by the laser pulse, but there was plenty else to witness – a scream of disbelieving terror, giving way to a paroxysm of coughing; a futile, panicked attempt to cover the helmet's breach with a gloved hand; a slump to the knees, scrabbling to grab hold, blind, of a gun that did not work; and a last pitch forward, servos still twitching—

Cory turned to his aunt, his arm actually raised. 'What the crap did you do that for? There was no need—'

'Cory, I was hot.'

He stared at her; didn't lower his arm.

'Oh, put that down,' she said. 'You should be able to appreciate, we cannot take prisoners. They certainly haven't.'

'This is—'

There was no time. The discordant whine of approaching engines, and the play of light, blue-green, fast-growing on the edge of the eastern ridge, spoke of trouble. They both turned to face the ridge. Cory untethered his gun – so far as he knew, it worked – and passed it to his aunt. Then he took the opportunity to urinate while there was yet a moment for such things.

Light was bad. Fast-moving was bad. Multiple engines was bad. And they were a good thirty metres from the closest cover – the quad-ski – in the ponderous suits. Teresa Maria gestured that they should move apart, which made sense... but so did falling back to the quad-ski. Cory started to turn—

The skid-bikes crested the ridge at speed. Three of them, one with a sidecar. *Four pharmhands*, Cory thought, hopes turning black. The sidecar's occupant was already firing. But not at Cory.

Teresa Maria, gun drawn, did not get to fire it. Five, six bursts of angry yellow erupted across her abdomen; she sank to her knees, dark liquid oozing out from the holes in her suit and quickly freezing on the icy surface in front of her. Something bright streaked just above Cory's head, and then he saw something else strike his aunt in the forearm—

'Cory—'

Enough, he told himself. *I'm not my aunt, but I'm not Arum either.*

'Alt ops axe Goldilocks,' he told the suit, wondering if the death warrant he'd just signed included his own.

He started acquiring targets. Two of the pharmhands were busy setting up a PMP, and one of the others was firing, of all things, a *crossbow*. The crossbow couldn't wait, because that looked seriously lethal, and the guy was quick-loading. Was in fact lifting his crossbow now, towards Cory. *Flash. Chill.* He ignored the arm-pain as best he could; it'd get worse. He loaded, and stored, the targeting on the two setting up the Personal Missile Platform, and then selected the visor on the printed-gun user, who had picked up the dropped crossbow and had started to lope towards where Teresa Maria still knelt on the ice, clutching at her guts.

Cory was no longer hot, but the laser didn't care. The laser would use whatever heat it could acquire, and he was still much, much warmer than Titan's ambient of minus one-seventy Celsius. *Flash. Chill.* Cory's arm felt as though it was snap-frozen, and he had taken out two pharmhands in ten seconds. The two at the PMP looked up, belatedly aware that the odds were perhaps no longer quite so golden. *Flash. Chill.* Cory gasped at astonishing pain, vowed he would not pass out. Could not raise his arm for several seconds.

The remaining pharmhand's visor took on a perfect-mirror finish. 'Alt ops target abort,' said Cory. The pharmhand returned its attention for the moment to the setup of the PMP, and Cory was wondering how to resolve the impasse when Teresa Maria again did it for him, via a crossbow bolt through the pharmhand's air-hose.

'But you took hits,' Cory said, his teeth now starting to chatter as his arm stole warmth from wherever it could get it. 'Several hits. I saw you bleeding out in the ice. And your arm—'

'Coolant,' explained Teresa Maria. 'And it wasn't my arm got hit, it was the *laser*. All up, I'm losing heat quite quickly right now – I suspect Ponnamperuna's going to be too long a haul, even on a skid-bike. But talking about arms, what the hell was that stunt you just pulled with yours?'

'It was an emergency, so I disabled the safety,' said Cory. 'There's nothing magical about body temperature, the suit would happily take us much lower than that, it's just that we wouldn't be happy with that. We like to stay in the Goldilocks zone – not too hot, not too cold. So Dayani built in a safety setting, which she had me code for – so, naturally enough, like any programmer, I put in an override, just in case. I was thinking it might put me hypothermic, but I guess the heat transfer rate was too slow for that – ended up getting frostbite like you wouldn't believe. Hopefully not hypothermia. Holy *shit*, that hurts.'

'Time's wasting. Can you ride?' asked Teresa Maria.

'Not with this arm, yet – think I'll need the sidecar. Sorry. I know that'll slow us down.'

'It'll still be faster than the quad-ski. And a crossbow bolt through the fuel cell will disable the other skid bikes – seems sensible. But we'd better move.'

'Think I know where. Mind if I navigate?'

*

'What is this place?' Teresa Maria asked. 'It's not on the charts.'

'I know,' replied Cory. They'd travelled south-south-west, then due east, for twenty minutes, putting almost twenty-five klicks between themselves and the killing ground. They were closer, significantly, to Neimann than to Ponnamperuna – but from the way Teresa Maria was hunched over the skid-bike's controls, they'd barely reached shelter in time.

Not out of the wilds yet, thought Cory. 'This place' was an unprepossessing old single-drum hab, rudimentary airlock, almost buried in the slope of a tall hydrocarbon-sand dune, on the fringe of one of Titan's lesser dune belts. Having keyed in a lengthy passcode on the airlock's modern-looking security plate, Cory fretted over trying to get the skid-bike in with them, but it wasn't going to happen: they were faced with the choice of leaving it out in the open, which wasn't ideal, and burying it in the dune, which presented its own problems. But first priority, he told himself, closing the airlock's outer hatch, was to get Teresa Maria warmed up and re-suited.

Through in the living quarters, it became clear that it was larger than a single-drum hab. There were excavations, living quarters for perhaps six or seven. Cory, still suited, fussed with the climate control, seeking to bring the environment up from Titan-ambient to a hospitable temperature. It wasn't instantaneous. The dry ice had not yet sublimed from the walls.

'Cory, what *is* this place?' Teresa Maria asked again, momentarily forgetting her thermal discomfort in the enigmatic surroundings of an unmapped habitat in the depths of northern Dilmun.

Her nephew, returning with a T-suit, replied, 'As far as I can make out, it's an abandoned mining operation from fifty years ago or so, but why it's not on the charts—'

'Lot of wildcatters back then. That could explain it. So how'd you find it?'

'I was out exploring with Arum, we came across it. And we – you know what Arum's like, not comfortable around people – we decided to use it as a getaway, a lot of the time, whenever she was in town.'

'Ah.'

There was too much worldly-wise understanding in that monosyllable for Cory's liking; he felt himself blushing furiously. 'Aunt Teresa,' he said, 'the hab should be almost warm enough now. To change.'

He carried suit, gloves, boots, liner – as much of it as possible in his left arm – and led Teresa Maria through into one of the private quarters. He'd shucked his own helmet by now. He hoped his aunt wasn't going to require help with removing her suit...

'So I presume this isn't *your* room,' she said.

Whether justly or no, he felt scandalised. To cover he remarked, as he retreated into the hab's central living area, 'I did come here on my own too. For peace and quiet. And privacy.'

'But you have an entire apartment in Ponnamperuna,' said Teresa Maria.

'That's not *true* privacy. When we were looking at bringing down the CREV, I needed to be sure that no-one was going to get word of what I was attempting. You don't get a second go at hacking a Cargo Re-Entry Vehicle out of orbit. So I knew I'd need a computer that wasn't compromised, had no chance whatsoever of being compromised. So I built one, here, and ensured that it never got connected to the net until I'd simulated the hack exhaustively, and I was *sure*. And it worked. And then I burnt the connection, so it couldn't be traced.'

'But, Cory, they *knew*,' said Teresa Maria. 'That dirigible was almost waiting for us. Did you tell Arum about the CREV?'

'No,' said Cory, 'and Arum wouldn't—'

'Someone did. Have you double-checked the computer?'

'I *told* you,' Cory said, almost shouting, 'I built it myself.'

'Which doesn't stop her adding something on without your knowledge,' Teresa Maria noted, having emerged from her changeroom. She rubbed the upper arms of her suit. 'How well do you really know her? Let me tell you straight up, Lex – Cory – you have *no idea what kind of baggage* people might be carrying. Even people in this room.'

'Aunt Teresa? What do you mean?'

'I mean people sometimes keep things about themselves from you for their own good, or for your own good, or for no good reason. You truly have no idea. Now you didn't find this place on your own, you say you found it one day when you were out exploring with *her*. And yet you maintain it's a perfectly safe, secure place from which to have planned a heist.'

'Aunt Teresa—' Cory began.

'She knew you hacked,' Teresa Maria persisted, her own voice raised, ragged. 'She was away from town more often than she was around, so what's that about? And I can't believe you watched her every moment she was here with you, so until you double-check the computer you just will not know. And she might well – wait, *that* sounded like an engine. Several engines.'

Cory stilled, straining to hear. There *had* been noise outside, but muffled by the confused acoustics of the hab's climate-control system. He dared not breathe, stared imploring at his aunt as, first, there came the crunch of boots on gritty ice and then the indistinct sound of voices from just outside the hab. A thud, clearer. At the airlock hatch. The boots retreated. Then quiet.

'*Put your helmet—*' Teresa Maria whispered urgently, then the front of the hab shook as the outer hatch blew.

fixing a hole

Hurtling just above an unwelcoming cold-poisoned sea, enveloped in Titanian night, the ekranoplan's cabin swerving and tilting unpredictably: both Portia and her stomach were distinctly unsettled. But Prof G, in his portly, homespun garb, and the pilot – Jungo something, or the like, a woman small and sharp enough to actually require the word *petite* – both seemed unfazed. So Portia determined to take her lead from them, and to accept as commonplace the vessel's rumbly, lazily-turbulent flight. And to ignore, as far as possible, that the other two seemed to be excluding her.

It wasn't something she found easy to ignore. The ekranoplan's cabin, ribbed and buttressed like the interior cavity of some biblical whale, was not large: most of the volume of a Mitsuda Skimmer's fuselage was allotted to insulation and cargo space, with the climate-controlled passenger compartment seemingly slotted in as an afterthought, just aft of the flight deck. And though there were viewports, they were small – ungenerous – and unsatisfying to peer through. Where the stubby, low-slung wings did not succeed in obscuring the view, the reflections from the craft's running lights bounced and slid off Kraken Mare's wave-disturbed surface, but could hardly be said to illuminate the murky sea over which they sped, much less the sky's light-swallowing, haze-canopied vastness. Looking through the grime-streaked viewport beside her, Portia couldn't even get a reliable sense of the horizon, other than a half-intellectual, half-instinctual awareness that it was much too close. She wished she'd been more persuasive in seeking to convince Prof G that a proper plane, or a proper boat, would have been immeasurably preferable to this too-low-flying, awkward half-hybrid; but the cost argument had been compelling. A charter would have been prohibitive; but the ekranoplan, on a regular cargo run from Zebker to the lodges on Mayda Insula, came at a tariff that would not raise questions with the grants-fund administrators (and this, as she was beginning to appreciate through Prof G's insistence on the subject – it was one of his 'pets' – was a consideration not to be taken lightly). Add in the opportunity to combine transport mode with data acquisition, by trailing the sonde through Kraken's upper layers as they flew, and the Skimmer had become the irresistible, inevitable option.

She could sit, and struggle to admire an almost-nonexistent view; she could seek to read or sim, and try not to fret over the disconcerting rattle of the craft's multiple electroprop engines; or she could join the not-quite-private conversation that the other two were holding in the flight deck. Some choice.

Nine hours: it was going to be a long flight. She wished she had realtime access to the sonde's data, but Severe Pilot Woman had been insistent that it be placed in 'batch' mode, so as not to transmit anything that might interfere with the Mitsuda's sense of self. So Portia would have to be content to analyse the results of the sonde's submerged run later, tomorrow perhaps, once they'd settled in at the chalet at Mayda.

It was always like this. She would be looking forward to something or other, would build up expectations, would have them crushingly unmet, subverted, tainted by some random intrusion. Such as, on this occasion, the discovery that Severe Pilot Woman was actually Prof G's sister-in-law… or, apparently, *ex*-sister-in-law. And so, where Portia had been anticipating an easy, meandering discussion of further research goals with Prof G, he'd instead deserted her in favour of re-establishing his acquaintance with the woman who'd left his brother. True, Prof G and the pilot did have age in common as well as a family history of some sort, on neither of which grounds could Portia compete as an equal. And true, she had no particular claim on Prof G herself, beyond the claim that any research subordinate has on her supervisor. But it still felt, to her, like a betrayal. And though she knew the feeling was unreasonable, it still rankled. Something always cropped up to spoil stuff.

Can't beat 'em, she thought, *can't escape them. May as well join 'em.* She unstrapped herself from the seat, stood up and wandered forward.

Prof G, in the co-pilot's seat, turned at her approach. 'Porsh, it's best that you remain seated.' She felt the words as a rebuke, though she knew that was probably not the intent. Prof G was just careful about the rules, was probably totally oblivious to the fact that his tone was belittling.

'No, she should be alright, Wiremu, long as she anchors herself to the support wall.' The pilot kept her eyes fixed on the plane's controls, and on the cockpit windscreen (which, unlike the viewports, evidently merited regular cleaning and thus spoke of genuine transparency). The expanse of Kraken immediately ahead of them shone white, edging to an almost unbelievably smooth grey. No waves showed ahead of those few that folded and stretched themselves around and beneath the ekranoplan's barely-airborne bow: the only waves on the whole of Kraken right now, she suspected, were those that the skimmer was transiently scribing across its surface. (Which made Portia wonder why the flight was not as perfectly smooth as the sea's surface itself.) In clipped, almost musically precise tones, the pilot asked, 'Can you see how to fit the webbing?'

Portia was a few seconds in realizing that the question had been directed at her. 'I think so,' she replied, moving to the wall just behind Prof G's seat and peeling out a net of elasticated straps from beside a see-through storage locker containing bottled water, dehydrated rations and a large thermos flask. She pressed her back against the auto-contouring surface of the bulkhead while she fastened the webbing across her chest and hips, breathing in sharply as it anaconda'd around her. She exhaled carefully, half afraid that the webbing was going to constrict further around her, but it appeared to have finished contracting. 'This supposed to be comfortable?' she asked.

'It's supposed to be *safe,*' replied the pilot – Junko Shaw, her namebadge revealed as she turned around in her seat. (What kind of a name was 'Junko', anyway?) Jet-black hair, bobbed; skin pale, with the first crease-marks of middle-age; sharp nose; piercing eyes. The brief smile now offered to Portia didn't reach those eyes. Portia got the feeling that not much did. Other than flight data, perhaps. The pilot turned back to face the front; Portia was left looking over the co-pilot's seat-back, and the sparsely-wisped dome of Prof G's head.

'So do you still see Todd?' Prof G asked. 'Not judging, just curious. I mean—'

'Yeah, no, not really. We both decided a clean break was best. At least, I think we both decided it,' said Junko. (Portia was surprised to note that the brusque precision had quite gone from the pilot's voice: so, then, an affectation. A defence mechanism?) 'And I certainly think it's been for the best.'

'How's Oaky taking it?'

'Oak*eh*,' said Junko. Evidently a correction, almost a reflexive one. 'Oh, he's... he's fine, I think. Now, anyway. It was difficult at first. He's at that age, you know?'

'Tell me about it,' answered Prof G. They both laughed briefly.

'Yours?' Junko asked.

Portia started to feel that she should disconnect the harness and return to her seat; she could see no way to make inroads into the conversation. But against this, something – whether it was being fully upright, or being able to see out the cockpit windscreen – had eased the upset in her stomach. Maybe she could abide a little more?

'Oh, they're...' Prof G paused. 'We're basically all good, I'd say. Arriette's about as well as can be expected at least, so there's that. And the lads are all—'

There was a jolt which made itself apparent both as a brief backwards pull and a distinct, dull thud. The ekranoplan's nose dipped. Junko's hands moved swiftly across the controls, and the craft bucked forward and upward... then seemed to slide back. Something towards the tail shook, there was a loud thump – *Jeez, I hope that wasn't the submersible*, Portia thought – and then the vehicle was level again, but no longer flying.

Swerving, skidding, still striving to surge forward, but no longer flying. Pressed awkwardly against the restraining straps, Portia rubbed a stinging elbow, and was alarmed to see a wave slap messily, and with Titan sluggishness, against the windscreen.

'Cock,' said Junko.

It seemed to sum things up well enough.

The engines were silent; the ekranoplan's forward motion had been arrested.

Junko had just re-emerged from the cargo hold airlock, holding a condensation-beaded T-suit helmet in one gloved hand and, in the other, a metre-long telescoped pole with a temperature sensor on its slender tip. She compressed the pole, dropped it into a thigh-pouch on her suit, then removed her gloves and stowed them neatly within the cavity of the helmet. She sat down heavily in the pilot's seat, her suit murmuring in protest. Placing the helmet at her feet, she worked the control panel to bring up, in one corner, a diagram of the Skimmer's underside.

'Are we sinking?' Portia asked, moving to get a decent view out of the cockpit's windscreen. Trying not to think about how many klicks lay between them and the shore. Trying to discount the sea's extreme, killing cold, held at bay only by battery-derived heat and a few layers of insulation. Trying not to wonder at the amber and red telltales currently blinking on the pilot's control panel. (And not, to any great extent, succeeding.)

'No,' said Junko. 'That's not the problem.'

But there is a problem, thought Portia. Her gaze strayed to Prof G – to Wiremu, as the pilot insisted on calling him – seeking some form of reassurance. She knew nothing of Junko's response to crisis: the woman exuded a distant, professional calm, which might or might not be trustworthy as a diagnostic of danger. But if Wiremu Garrity wasn't alarmed, then Portia needn't be, either.

Prof G looked worried.

135

'We do seem,' he said – appearing to choose each word with care, using the tone Portia knew all too well from academic meetings – 'to be riding lower in the liquid than we were before takeoff.'

'Yes, we are,' said Junko, without lifting her gaze from the controls. 'There's been a breach of some sort in the underside. Here.' She tapped at a spot on the control panel's diagram, more-or-less amidships, and a gently pulsating orange circle obediently blossomed into existence on the display. 'Right at the anchorage point for your sonde. Just the fuselage's outer skin, obviously, not the inner layer, or we'd have worse problems. We're not in any danger of losing actual buoyancy, the cargo hold itself hasn't been breached, and I couldn't smell anything to worry about when I cracked the helmet, but with the amount of liquid we're taking on in the hullspace, it does mean we can't get airborne again. Which is why I killed the engines. Plus I've activated the emergency beacon, which Mayda's acknowledged. So now, as I see it, we sit tight and wait for help to arrive. We've got rafts, of course, but frankly we're better just staying put until we get picked up.'

'How long is that likely to take?' Portia asked, wishing her voice didn't sound so small.

'A day, perhaps. Hopefully not longer.'

'A *day*? But you said Mayda's acknowledged already.'

'We're just about at Kraken's midpoint, which puts us around six hundred klicks from the nearest assistance, and the initial response is just an automated callback. We're in the system, but I don't know more than that at this stage. Right now, I'm guessing, Zebker, Westlake, and Mayda are arguing over who's best placed to reach us, with the vehicles they have on hand. My bet is that Mayda will send out a launch, something with enough range for the return trip – which rules out any of their aircraft, they're just shore-skimmers for the tourists – and enough towing capacity to handle us. But we're pretty much in the wilds up here, and help isn't exactly close. It will take as long as it takes, and the best we can do is just sit tight in the interim.'

There was an undercurrent, Portia thought, to Junko's words – or rather, to their delivery. A forced casualness, a making light.

There's something she's not letting on. She's reassured us on the buoyancy. But I notice she hasn't mentioned heat loss. How long can the ekranoplan's power reserves hold up against immersion, even partial immersion, at liquid-nitrogen temperatures? Isn't it starting to feel cold in here already?

A day might well be a long ask. She searched the side of the pilot's face for an answer to the question she dared not raise.

'Any idea what caused it?' Prof G asked. 'I mean, the sonde, obviously, somehow, but… I wouldn't have envisaged there'd be anything for it to snag on.'

'There isn't,' replied Junko. 'That's to say, this is probably the most well-established flightpath across Kraken, that's why we use it. Other than the throat itself, and we're a good hour past that, there's no exposed terrain, no seamounts… nothing shallower than twenty-five metres for an entire thirteen-hundred-klick stretch, and most of it's much deeper than that. Your sonde was on a six-metre tether, and we were at an altitude of between two and three metres, so no, I don't see how it could have struck anything. The flightpath's barred to shipping—'

'Ice?' Portia asked.

'Kraken doesn't get ice,' the pilot answered. 'You might get some hydrocarbon ice in Ponga this deep into winter, because it's much further north. But even then, it'd be mainly around the shoreline. And never solid enough, thick enough, to shear off something the way the sonde must've been ripped off. And it's supposed to be the tether that gives first. *Not* the fuselage.'

'Can't we look at jury-rigging some kind of repair? I mean, can you pump out the hullspace?' asked Prof G, in what Portia recognised as his dangerous I-have-an-idea tone of voice.

'Yes, we can pump it,' said Junko, a trace of weariness showing in her voice. 'But from the speed at which Kraken's leaked in, it's a sizeable hole, possibly even most of a panel. A small puncture, anything up to four or five centimetres across, we can handle. But we've got no real way that I can think of to repair a larger breach.'

'But if we could repair the fuselage somehow – say, with a custom-printed patch – we could pump out the liquid and potentially get airborne again?'

'In principle,' Junko conceded. 'But we'd need a programmable industrial fabricator to print such a thing.'

'We're shipping a fabricator to Mayda,' Prof G answered. 'Not a particularly large one, admittedly, but I think we have enough source material to replace a panel. We're talking what, a square metre of hull? You'll have the specs in memory somewhere, for that section of the underside?'

'Well, yes,' said Junko. 'But without any way of visually inspecting the damage, it wouldn't be possible to design something to fit it exactly. I didn't get the impression, from the thermal trace of the cargo hold's floor, that it was anything so neat and tidy as just an entire panel sheared off.'

'That's OK; we can check that. And it should be possible to design something that will just lock into place against the damage. It should be more-or-less self-sealing.'

'But we can't inspect the hole!' Junko complained, sounding more than a little exasperated at Prof G's seemingly-unshakeable confidence. (Portia could sympathise with that.) 'I mean, I know the approximate location from the thermal trace, but that's as blurred as bug—'

'We have a miniature submersible rigged up for sensing.' Prof G held his hands out, about forty centimetres apart, just above the control panel. 'It'll still need someone to baby it, but we can get it to provide a detailed scan of the hole.'

Junko turned to look at her ex-brother-in-law, a look of – Portia guessed – puzzlement in her eyes. 'Just what kind of business are you and Petra up to at Mayda?'

'Portia,' Prof G corrected automatically, then offered a small, precise grin. 'Let's just say we're hunting buried treasure.'

'Asteroidal minerals?' Junko asked. Metals were rare anywhere on Titan's surface, and keenly sought.

'In essence, yes,' said Prof G.

'Lucrative,' Junko remarked, her eyes still narrow. 'Bit of a change from astrophysics, though, isn't it?'

If you only knew, thought Portia, bursting to tell.

'It keeps us busy,' said Prof G, with that grin again.

'So this submersible you mention... it's not manned,' Junko said.

'Oh, no. Much too small.' Prof G again made the 'fish this big' gesture.

'RC, then?'

'Line-of-sight only, at this stage. The full comms rig comes later, this trip is supposed to be just a depth test under field conditions. So it needs a handler, close by.'

'That's a problem then, given that we're currently steeped in minus-two-hundred Celsius. I mean, we've got T-suits, obviously—' Junko picked up the helmet for emphasis, '—but survival time, immersed, in a T-suit—'

'We can do a bit better than a T-suit, too,' said Prof G, and Portia's heart sank a little further at the almost-boastful assuredness in his tone, because she sensed what was coming next. '*We've* brought a lakesuit.'

Yes, we've brought a lakesuit. But which of us is it, Prof G, who'll be required to use it?

She knew the answer to that one already.

It had been possible, while Portia had been climbing into the suit, to take some comfort from its substantiality, from the robustness of its construction. Now, though, standing beside the T-suited Junko, and faced with the dark immenseness of the liquid that lapped at the airlock's lower lip, that comfort was a thing past. Acutely conscious of the sound of her own breathing, the shudder of her own heart, she could not convince herself that there was any sort of limit to the sea's expanse: she would step onto the ekranoplan's barely-submerged left wing, then into the sea's depths, and that would simply be the end of her. Swallowed, enveloped, annulled.

Crazy. You've done dives. You can do this... But those had been small lakes, in daylight, where the lakebed had been at just four or five metres' depth. This was the long polar winter night, and Kraken, at a point where the seabed might conceivably be as much as three hundred metres beneath her. And the lakesuit was not positively buoyant. If some problem developed with the safety line (synthetic warmrope) that tethered her suit's backframe to the airlock's stanchion, if the suit's emergency float failed as had been known to happen, she would fall. And fall. And nobody would be able to do anything about it.

It's all very well for Prof G. He's not the one risking his life out here. But he'd offered her the choice of refusal, and she hadn't taken it.

'If there's any kind of problem, if you need to be hauled up, just give a tug on the line.'

'Got it,' Portia answered.

'You're sure you're up for this?' Junko asked her.

No. 'Yes.'

'Then we'd best get busy.'

Portia hefted the little robot submersible, checked that it was synched to the control keypad embossed on her suit's left wrist, and double-checked the fastenings at each terminus of the rope umbilical that connected the submersible to her hip. She'd dialled down the heating in this rope so that it would be only barely flexible once the cold of Kraken bit in: less cord, more rod. It would give her a bit more control over the submersible's position, should speed the process up some.

'Immersion will drain the safety line pretty quickly,' Junko advised her. 'You'll only have a few minutes' pliancy before it gets too cold and brittle, so don't waste time down there.'

Wasn't planning to, thought Portia. 'Got it,' she said again, hoping she sounded confident. *This is madness. And I'm not ready... but I'm never going to be ready.*

She forced herself to step down, onto the wing, then into the chilled abyss.

*

Heart thumping, she felt herself fall into the unknown: two seconds, three, and then the safety line jerked at her back.

The chill was expected. It was always the noise that surprised her, each time she dived – though she imagined she'd grow accustomed to it if she did it often enough. The low growling hiss of it, as the sea's liquid effervesced against the warmer casing of the lakesuit. Bubbles fogged the outside of her helmet's viewplate, smudging out, for several seconds, all but the most rudimentary sense of her surroundings, which gradually seeped back into existence: the uncertain and seemingly distant glow of the ekranoplan's running lights, the ghost of her own, upraised, helm-lamp-illuminated hand, awkwardly reaching out to help her impose a visual scale on the fuzzy vista above her. The disorientation was something that would last only for a half-minute or so, until her vision cleared sufficiently; easy enough to talk yourself through it, in the context of a test-dive in some small, shallow, tame body of liquefied methane, less easy when the seabed was unguessably distant beneath her. The lakesuit could keep her alive much longer, submerged, than would a standard T-suit; even so, were the safety line to grow brittle and shatter in response to a failure of its heating system, she might well be dead from heat-loss or from suit failure even before she reached the seafloor.

Electric warmth still bloomed from the fingers of her gloves: her hands continued to hiss bubbles. But already the joints of her suit had grown painfully cold and the viewplate, while still fogged, was probably as close to transparency as she could afford for now. She'd best get busy. She pushed the little robot away towards the nebulous, irregular shape of the breach in the fuselage's underside, a metre or two above her.

'Coffee?' Junko asked her, while Prof G busied himself with porting the surveillance record from the submersible's memory to the fabricator.

Portia was about to decline the offer, then reconsidered. If nothing else, the warmth would be welcome. Despite all the thermal defences of the lakesuit, the cold had bitten deep into her limbs, and her teeth were chattering, even from just a five-minute immersion. 'Thanks,' she answered.

She'd kept the lakesuit on (save the helmet and gloves) – she'd be needing it soon enough. The cabin's air had frosted on it when she'd first emerged from the airlock; now, as the suit warmed, the frost turned to dew, and lazy rivulets of condensation ran down the casings of her legs. She hoped the cabin's flooring was sufficiently well-sealed that she wasn't dripping on anything crucial.

'Got it,' said Prof G. 'Think so, anyway. You want to check this, Porsh? You understand this contraption's idiosyncrasies better than I do.'

She moved closer. 'Did you set it for cryo?'

'How d'you mean?' he asked.

She leaned over the fabricator, forgetting to be concerned about moisture from the suit. 'If you just construct something at room T, it'll be shrunken by a fraction of a percent once you get down to minus two hundred, and that'll mean that it won't actually fit properly at ambient temperature. You can correct for that here, by setting the reference temperature.'

'Glad you told me,' he replied.

She was glad too – it always felt good to be useful, and to demonstrate that she did indeed have a level of technical expertise that complemented the Prof's grasp of theory. 'You'll also need to make sure that the structure's happy to deform itself the right way, as it cools. There are routines under the cryo menu that will help with that, to give a flexible lattice microstructure. That way you can make it thicker, and stronger too, than if it was simply solid.' She watched to ensure that he was doing as she advised – *role reversal*, she thought, *better savour the moment* – and went off to collect the coffee that she could smell over the suit's strange, sweet, brackish whiff of lake-taint.

Behind her, the fabricator was warming up, ready to move into production. They could make the part they needed for repair; this might well not be the full disaster it had first appeared. (Of course, someone still had to *fit* it...)

Ping. Ping. Ping... ping. As if on cue, a short series of metallic stress notes from the direction of the ekranoplan's rear got everyone's attention. Prof G, looking up from the fabricator, raised his eyebrows at Junko.

'Hold's cooling,' she responded, with enough of an edge to that verdict that Portia didn't doubt its implications.

The craft was buoyant only by virtue of its air-filled compartments, which were likely to suffer cryogenic depressurisation (and, therefore, possible rupture) as the chill cut in. If the cargo hold's temperature, and therefore pressure, dropped sufficiently that it was no longer able to withstand the thicker Titanian atmosphere, it would leak, and a leak anywhere towards the floor of the hold would ensure that it took in liquid from Kraken. And if it took in liquid from Kraken...

The fabricator's mechanical lack of urgency, as it patiently constructed a component that might be completed too late to be of use, could yet doom them all.

Portia's hands, in the well-heated gloves, were close enough to warm; the rest of her, legs in particular, were starkly cold. The repair panel, which was now fitted all-but-flush into the wound in the ekranoplan's underside like some bizarrely-designed jigsaw piece, still required just a couple of nudges – *percussive maintenance*, as Prof G would describe it – to ensure that the farthest corner was properly wedged within the hull's rent, for an effective seal. Portia stretched, fingertips pushing out in vain: the errant corner remained stubbornly out of reach.

She'd need a tool of some sort, to increase her arm's span. There was a gripper in the suit's pouch, wasn't there? She pushed her free hand into the pouch, rummaged clumsily, and emerged several seconds later with the gripper: just twenty centimetres long, but it would serve. Not bothering to loop its tether-chain around her wrist, she stretched out with the gripper, gingerly tapping at the still-protruding corner of the repair patch. *Not helping that much. Need to put a bit more force behind it. But it's difficult to see clearly through the fogged visor. And I'm wary of hitting it too hard.*

On the third strike, she dropped the tool. Grabbed for it, missed. Lunged, stretched, knocked it further away, to her side. Behind her, something gave. She angled herself down and stretched her arm wide, to better reach the slowly-descending gripper. Caught it.

Turned around, reached up.

She was no longer tethered to the Skimmer. The safety line had cleaved off from the anchoring clasp that, presumably, was still attached to her suit's backframe. She could see the rope trailing above her, still flexing, mockingly just out of reach.

She strove to claw her way towards the surface, and safety; but the gear that kept her alive, in the suit, also kept her heavy, in a liquid appreciably less dense than water. And the lakesuit was not designed for the degree of bodily movement required for swimming.

She tried, in increasing desperation; but she could not regain the rope.

Letting go of the urgency which had not availed her, she felt herself subtly falling, into Kraken's hypercold, good-as-fathomless depths.

The blood in her ears like static, the futile surge of adrenaline, the sudden thunder of her heart, the taste of bile.

The naked dread, and atop it all the self-recrimination. *Stupid, stupid, stupid!*

She flailed. She swore. She yelled.

She felt the pressure build behind her eyes, the awful tightness across her chest.

She lost perhaps five metres to the tussle between panic and despair before her training kicked in. *The float.*

She tried to remember the steps involved in activating and releasing the suit's emergency float. *Panel, lower left torso – need to twist it off. Lift out the float assembly. Then open the valve.* She'd done it in drills, but that had been without the chemicals of fear insistently pulsing through her system. It took her – how many seconds? How many metres? She did not like to think – to get the panel off. More time, more time she didn't fucking *have,* with unworkably clumsy fingers, to extract the float: a collapsed buoy, tethered by a chain to her suit's framework and by a cryoprotected gas line to the valve inset into the suit's torso. And then the valve refused to turn, despite all the force of her desperation. She continued to drop. She didn't dare look up, afraid of what she might see. Or not see.

And all the while she fell, at such a sedate pace that it seemed Kraken was toying with her. Which was incorrect, of course: Kraken simply didn't care. (And – with radio comms to the Skimmer piggybacked onto the safety line – those who did care, helpless and however-many-metres above, might not even know yet of her predicament, beyond perhaps wondering at her lack of a response to them.)

The descent into darkness and killing chill: Kraken as Ultima Thule.

The valve refused to budge. *Fucking typical.*

No, wait…

Anticlockwise! In turning it the wrong way, she'd overtightened it, and now it would not loosen. The cold didn't help, nor did the gloves. *Shift!*

Finally, the valve turned. Helium began to flow; the inflating buoy twitched and pulled like a fish on a line.

My luck if it bursts. Or if it breaks the chain.

But it didn't. The buoy began to ascend, and pulled taut on its chain. Then, still swelling, it brought her descent to a stop. And started to rise.

Only then, heart still thudding against her ribs, did she dare to look at the depth gauge on her right wrist. *Forty-four metres. Fuck me.*

Forty-three. Forty-two. Forty.

The helium was certainly doing its job. The buoy was going to make a significant splash when it reached the surface.

Except that, as it turned out, it didn't quite reach the surface. The Skimmer's hull got in the way.

The collision was audible through her suit, a low-pitched clatter with enough of a crunch about it that Portia knew, instantly, that it was nothing so benign and so inconsequential as a simple ricochet. The buoy hadn't fared too well from the impact, was leaking like a slow-boiling kettle, but that was far from the worst of it.

The lakesuit appeared not to be harmed, but maybe it would have been kinder if it were.

She took one look at the new damage to the repair patch, and gloom slammed down on her like a shutter, even as she reached out to the once-more-accessible safety line.

Stupid, stupid, stupid, she told herself.

Junko, T-suited, was waiting for her in the airlock; sought to restrain her when she tried to remove the lakesuit too early in the lock's cycle. Portia could not stop herself from shaking, could not bring herself to look at the other woman's faceplate. Her own visor was still smeared with a light frosting of hydrocarbon gunk, residue from the now-evaporated methane and nitrogen that principally comprised the liquid bulk of Kraken; but the shaking was not from cold, and the lack of eye contact did not derive from the obscuration of her viewplate. She was shocked witless by what had just happened out there.

At the earliest moment she dared, she pulled her helmet off: the lock's air still stank of Kraken, sick-sweet-sharp-burnt, and stung with chill. She coughed, startled, and fought the impulse to gag. 'I wrecked it,' she confessed, only barely stopping herself from wiping her eyes with her still-frosted gloves. 'Jesus. I mean, I had it almost right, and I lost it out there, and it's *wrecked.*'

Junko cracked her own helmet's seal, stared at her, reached an arm across to the other's shoulder. Her grip was surprisingly hard. 'Portia, calm. Calm. You did your best.'

My 'best' has just probably sealed our fate.

Even if they had enough raw material to print another supplemental repair patch, the process would very probably take more time than they had, and would use valuable power that was already stretched thin between heating, life support, and the reserves that were needed for flight. And the longer they needed to heat the ekranoplan's passenger cabin against Kraken's killingly-cold liquid, the less reserves would remain to power them towards Mayda…

It was all a moot point, anyway. With the hull still pierced, they couldn't keep the hullspace pumped out, couldn't reduce weight enough to get airborne. Several thousand litres of liquid methane were pinning them down.

Junko cycled the lock's inner hatch, and led her back into the passenger cabin, which Portia was alarmed to note had acquired a slight rearward slope. *That can't be good.*

Prof G turned in his seat, the smile on his face thin and dying abruptly as he caught sight of Portia's visage. Some signal of the eyes passed between him and the pilot. 'What happened?' he asked softly.

I fucked up, Prof G. I fucked up. 'The buoy,' she said. 'It rammed the patch. So we're still shipping Kraken.' She sighed, started pulling off her gloves. Forced a smile, even though she really didn't have it in her. 'Bright side, I can confirm that the suit holds down to forty, at least.'

'You fell to *forty metres?*' he asked. 'Portia, I'm just very relieved you're OK.'

But I'm not OK. None of us are. We're going to die here. 'We're still breached,' she reminded him, forcefully, almost angrily.

'You say that. But *how* breached? Do we need to replace the whole panel?'

A part of her could almost admire his academic persistence, his insistence on looking for a solution. But a larger part was just disappointed with herself and frustrated at his inability to see that no reasonable solution existed, and it was this part of her that answered him. She forced herself to sound professional, measured. 'No, it looked like only a corner was broken off. Maybe ten centimetres' diameter or so. Still enough to amount to too much of a leak. But *Prof...* the last time around, it took us two hours to survey the damage, design the patch, print it... and then it still needed to be installed.' She looked pointedly at Junko, then at the professor, then gestured at the sloping floor, waved to indicate the rear of the passenger cabin. 'You telling me you think we still *have* two hours before Kraken claims us for good?'

'I'm not inclined to give up while there's any hope for repair,' Prof G countered. 'Let's look at the resources we have available.'

Not enough time, thought Portia.

'Not enough power,' said Junko, who had moved through to the cockpit and was now poring over the controls. 'I hate to say it, Wiremu, but Portia's right. We don't have enough reserves to stave off the cold, to print a repair, to pump the hull, and then to get us airborne and to Mayda. And the cargo hold is failing progressively – ultimately, it won't just be Titan's air that leaks in, it'll be Kraken itself, and I suspect that'll happen well before the Mayda launch can get here – they're still over nineteen hours away, on present estimates. Our best bet now, and by 'best' I mean 'least worst', is to suit up and deploy a raft.'

She knows full well a raft won't insulate us against – what? – twenty hours or so on Kraken, before help arrives. It's just death delayed.

'Well, if it's as hopeless as that,' Prof G said, 'then I'm at least going to have another coffee before I climb into that suit. I just think we must be missing something – surely there must be *something* that we can use as an emergency sealant of some kind?'

A sealant? Portia caught sight of the thermos flask, and a wild idea struck her. 'Maybe there is,' she said.

Tethered to the airlock's stanchion by two six-metre safety lines, she stepped back into the sea and waited for the helmet-fogged blindness to pass.

Ten seconds… twenty… thirty… Then she helped Junko to lower the heavy, awkward shape of Prof G's T-suit – also tethered – into Kraken. While she hefted the lifeless T-suit into a more-or-less upright position beside her, and waited for the first bloom of its effervescence to dissipate, she retrieved the knife from her lakesuit's storage pouch.

The knife was tethered, too, to Portia's wrist. (No point in taking chances.) The knife was not overly sharp – less chance of an inadvertent puncture – nonetheless, it should be enough to break the chill-brittled skin of the water-filled T-suit, and expose its precious fluid cargo to Kraken's murderous cold.

She looked up at the fuzzed silhouette of the ekranoplan's underside just above her. *Lucky thing it was the near corner of the repair patch that got punctured by the buoy, otherwise it'd be well out of reach for this.*

Portia's original notion had been that she would take the thermos with her down into Kraken… but the thermos had only a one-litre capacity, and none of them had been able to think of a satisfactory way of propelling the water from the thermos into the breach in the hull.

But when you thought about it, a thermos flask was just a device for keeping its contents at a temperature distinct from that of its surroundings. Much like a T-suit… and T-suits were designed, within limits, with flexibility in mind. They could be bent; distorted; compressed.

Against Kraken's cryogenic temperatures, even the T-suit's thermal defences would not keep the eighty litres of water warm, nor even liquid, for long. But provided Portia could puncture the suit quickly enough, and could apply sufficient force to squeeze out enough of its quick-setting contents towards the hole in the ekranoplan's repair patch, it just might work. Elbow would be best, they'd decided: the fabric there was more flexible than the knee, and she could work the arm like a bellows, to extrude the water out like quick-setting sealant.

Time to get it done. Holding the T-suit a little away from her like a dance partner, she wielded the knife.

'Pumps are still making progress,' announced Portia, strapping herself in. 'Hull-space is almost drained out.'

'Excellent improvisation, Porsh,' said Prof G, turning to face her. 'Even if it has been at the expense of a perfectly decent T-suit. Mercedes herself couldn't have done better.'

'Thanks, Wiremu,' Portia replied, rankling just a little at the mention of her supervisor's previous postdoc. *Way to spoil the moment, Prof G.* But she coloured with pride, nonetheless.

'Think this duck will make it to Mayda?' Prof G asked.

'Time to find out,' Junko replied, from the pilot's seat.

The throaty hum of the engines – throb, rattle, and all – was the sweetest sound Portia could imagine.

The ekranoplan leapt forward.

phlashback

'You've killed them.' Arum's words were quiet, her voice bleak.

They'd e-locked the arms and legs on her T-suit. Her limbs, aching from the residue of the dull *fleet* comedown, could not be shifted. The ground's deep chill advanced up from her feet.

'Killed? I've merely clarified their choices,' the officer explained. *Arrogant prick.* He muttered something, on another channel, to the guard whose weapon covered her. As though her immobilisation weren't sufficient containment.

Two of the T-suited mil figures had moved in around the dune-buried hab's half-breached airlock. One picked up some of the larger shards of C-fibre plating from the blown hatch; the other, holding a flat piece of ordnance, stood to the side.

Arum watched the spotlit activity around the ragged-shadowed hatch. She took in the churning dust around the ruined hatch, the methane-damp sand at the hab's base puddled with new shrapnel. She felt a growing, sapping sense of helplessness. The temptation was strong to drawdown on her metabolism's last reserves of *steel*, but how could that help? Bluntly put, it couldn't, even disregarding her locked suit.

Four mil personnel, five if you counted the transport's pilot, all armed. Plus eight more captive pharmhands – who now would never trust her again, and were therefore best accounted amongst the tally of opponents – back in the flarecraft's cabin. Biomet enhancement was no benefit against those odds.

Any resistance, any hint of trouble from her, right now, would merely hasten the deaths of Cory and his aunt… and herself.

The officer turned to glance back towards the glare of the waiting transport's searchlights; Arum had no idea what he sought.

He spoke again. 'Pagnell. Route a channel through the hab's alarm system. Jakande. Limpet the inner hatch. Three-minute fuse. Activate on my mark.'

'Ready,' the soldier with the limpet control advised after far too short an interval. She stepped several paces back from the airlock. Her comrade followed.

'Mark,' the officer announced. He part-turned to Arum. 'Persuade them,' he told her, his voice carrying that private-channel buzz. 'They come out with hands raised, weapons discarded, or we fire.' He raised his gloved hand, three fingers extended. 'Use the time wisely.'

She tried to extract herself from the *fleet* hangover, and from her sudden surprise that they had unlocked her suit; tried to marshal an argument. A plea. The words wouldn't come.

'Cory,' she said at last, too softly, not knowing how much time she'd wasted. Not knowing if she had an audience at all. Louder: 'Cory, please come out. Hands raised. The mil have given an assurance you won't be harmed.' She stared into the visor on the officer's beige-and-rust camo'd helmet, seeking to read the truth of that assurance, but the mirrored surface gave no hint. Nor, too, were there any answers to be found in the glare-shielded shape of the transport, squatting like a toad on its supports, nor in the night-deep darkness surrounding the vehicle's harsh cone of illumination. 'Cory, please come out. They've given you three minutes. It's over.' It wasn't enough, she knew it wasn't, but what more could she say? *I'm sorry, truly sorry?* There was a time for that, but under armed guard and flat-empty from pharm's aftereffects wasn't it.

The seconds dripped away. She could find no new words. Her limbs ached from the residue of the dull *fleet* comedown, from stress, from exhaustion. The airlock hatch remained impassive.

She waited, helpless.

The flarecraft's cabin stank, stale sweat and gasoline. The chilled air rang with the whine of the transport's engines. The flarecraft's flight could hardly have been more lumpy if they'd been on the ground. Still, Arum supposed she should be grateful they'd got it airborne: it was certainly laden.

Sixteen seats, two rows, facing across the transport's passenger cabin. Three of the end seats were occupied by guards; eleven others by captives such as herself and Cory, their suits e-locked, their helmets held against their chests or balanced precariously on laps. They were packed in well beyond Arum's comfort levels; she had to fight to keep her gorge down. Nothing new there, except the lack of strategies she could adopt to escape the sense of looming crisis, of confinement. Crammed in like freight, Arum yearned for the sense of freedom that solitude, or a sealed suit, could provide.

All of the pharmhand captives, herself included, were camo-T-suited, in imitation of the mil guards' enhanced suits; Teresa Maria's T-suit was civ-standard, visibility blue; Cory was still in his bulky and now rather battered nightsuit. She was surprised they'd let him keep that on, in place of a regular suit. They must be in a hurry.

Or maybe they didn't realise.

Cory looked half-dead, beaten by circumstance. Slumped, his eyes nearly closed, a large bruise on the side of his head just starting to discolour. He was cradling his arm – his right arm, his laser arm – as though it were broken, and every so often he winced as he attempted to raise or lower it. Faced with a handmade suit that wouldn't recognise their servo-blockers, the mil personnel had settled for lashing duropolymer restraints across him. Not that he looked as though he had any fight left in him, anyway. Cory looked more spent than anyone else in the cabin.

He wouldn't acknowledge her. No grunted response; no slight inclination of the head; no eye contact. Nothing. After a couple of minutes, she gave up, trying to keep the pain from her face. Swallowing when she needed to.

She didn't even bother trying to attract the attention of Teresa Maria, seated beside Cory and one space down across from Arum. His aunt, who had limped markedly on the short walk to the flarecraft, looked every bit as exhausted as Cory did. Or almost every bit: there was a residue still, in her eyes, of the cornered predator.

The flight droned, and shook, and droned. Heads nodded, whether from simple fatigue or enhancement hangover or both, some resting chins or cheeks awkwardly against their suits' neck-flanges. Others turned, stared, glowered. Teresa Maria was doing her share of that. So was the pharmhands' primary hard man, Reid, seated on Cory's other side, his cheek scraped red where he'd been rifle-butted earlier as an object lesson to those who hadn't understood the guards' 'no verbal' command. Cory, between them, drooped in his suit. He nodded forward, whispered distractedly against his suit's neck-rim. Once again she sought to attract his attention, risking the guards' ire. It was fruitless: Cory didn't respond. He looked out of it.

The cabin lacked windows. There was no way to track time, location, speed, or altitude: that was all in the helmet on her lap. Still, it was most likely that the flarecraft was running the mostly-level gap between dunes; the vehicle's performance atop sloping sand would be poor. Dune-running would bring the flarecraft out around fifty klicks southwest of Neimann. Assuming they then took the most direct route, they'd be fifteen minutes out of the big mil base at Neimann once they turned.

Those last fifteen minutes would be the most precarious. For now, the flarecraft's low flight was largely masked by the flanking dunes. That would change.

The seconds slid away. She felt, as always, the treacherous pull of pharmhand biomet enhancements, but let them lie. She wasn't sure what she'd need to survive once the flight had ended. Or how long she'd do so.

Was it getting colder? Not that complaint to their captors would serve any purpose or win any favours. It was a fair bet that the mil would have worse lined up for the pharmhands back at Neimann.

There was condensation on the chestplate of Cory's nightsuit. Condensation, transforming to frost.

She lifted her gaze, desperate to find something neutral to look at. If they twigged—

She fumbled the helmet on her lap, half-dropped it, bent to secure it in her gloves, leaning forward enough to subvoke a four-word command into its rim. Forced her eyes to cross for three seconds: a precise biomet signal. As she leaned back against her seat, she convulsed, doubled over as far as her locked suit would permit, vomited into the helmet on the lap of the pharmhand directly across. 'Sorry,' she mumbled, yellow drool still dripping from the corner of her mouth.

'Clumsy *bitch*!' Fateh glared at her, dropped the fouled helmet, snatched Arum's own helmet from her lap.

Cory still hadn't emerged from his slumber. Had they dosed him?

Sweat was streaming down the sides of his ruddying face. As long as nobody noticed the growing patches of ice on his suit...

'Hey!' said Reid, and made to pull himself away from Cory's side. *Damn.* A dozen pairs of eyes turned in his direction. Two of the guards started pulling themselves to their feet, reaching for weapons. This was going to go bad.

Now, *now*, she needed *steel*. She pressed her tongue, hard, against the roof of her mouth, as far back as could be reached. Held it, three painfully-long seconds, until she felt the pharm flow.

Called out, as loud as she could, 'Cory! Hands up! Now!'

Cory's emergence from heat-stress slumber was almost too late. Arum couldn't even be sure he'd read the situation before, half-aimed, his suit's laser had pulsed blindingly towards the flarecraft's cockpit. Her vision chaotic with sudden afterimages, she couldn't tell what the UV pulse had hit. But she could smell smoke.

The vehicle's nose dropped almost instantly. A deafening klaxon cut through the air. The two mil guards, well out of their seats, were too preoccupied with retaining their footing to attempt other action in the couple of seconds preceding impact; those seated focussed on getting their helmets on. Arum took advantage of the confusion, and of the short-lived strength that *steel* lent her, to wrest a clean helmet out of her neighbour's gloved hands. She had almost succeeded in slotting the helmet in place when—

The air smelled diseased, felt cold. Not a good sign.

She'd been out to it. Her neck ached. Her eyes wouldn't unblur. Pain all down her left side; blood in her mouth.

Arum could tell the cabin was filled with noise. But she could hear nothing above her ears' ringing.

She was askew, still firmly strapped in her seat: the cabin was at a sharp angle. The landing had been brutal.

She must've blacked out in the crash.

She'd dropped the helmet. The burnt-sand-and-wax smell told her she'd need one, sooner rather than later. The *steel* in her veins strained to slip the leash. She unstrapped, tried to stand, almost fell across the aisle.

'Cory?' she asked, the sound scarcely audible against the insistent, grating klaxon. Someone groaned. Didn't sound like Cory.

The *steel* had brought her back to consciousness before the other passengers, but its edge wouldn't last long. And the factory reset she'd initiated, just before the crash, hadn't yet brought her suit back online: unlocked, but not yet awake.

Vision improved, enough to suggest that one mil guard and two pharmhands were dead in their seats, killed either by the impact itself or struck by untethered gear or personnel. Cory was next along that row of seats, and he wasn't moving.

One of the cabin's remaining two guards was trying to right herself. If she reached her weapon before Arum got there—

Arum stood, pushed the guard aside towards a half-risen pharmhand; the two went down in a heap.

Steel was great... while it lasted. She grabbed the guard's gun, latched it to her hip, looked around for the other weaponry that must exist; no sign. *No time.*

Her suit, at least, was functioning properly now. And someone in the cockpit was evidently sufficiently conscious to kill the klaxon.

Cory's helmet, where is Cory's helmet? If she couldn't find that, there was no point continuing.

Find it later. She directed an elbow jab and a kick at another pharmhand struggling to rise from his seat, then set to removing Cory's tethers. They would take too long to untie; she simply snapped them. Found his helmet at his feet, lifted it. Then placed her other hand on Cory's arm, ready to pull him up.

Cory's face was red, sweat-sheened. As things went, that was a good sign.

Teresa Maria latched a proprietary hand on Cory's other arm, turned balefully to Arum. 'Haven't you done *enough* damage?' she asked, in a voice thick with hatred.

Arum was all for leaving Teresa Maria to her fate, but she was certain that that wouldn't play well. 'I'm saving Cory,' she replied. 'You can join us, or you can stay. But I intend to survive.' She pulled Cory up towards her, wincing at his evident pain.

Pain was Nature's way of reminding you that you still lived. Arum's body would remember that, soon enough, when the *steel* wore off.

Teresa Maria rose groggily after Cory.

'I can get you out,' Arum explained to them, 'but you'll need to follow my lead.' *And hope none of the other pharmhands is still packing biomet.* She passed Cory his helmet, picked up the one she'd vomited in – messy, but it was the only way to be sure it wasn't her own standard-issue camo lid – and tipped the worst of the mess out before donning it. Whispered a two-word code. Then she started moving towards the cabin's front, and the exit, without waiting to see that the other two had sorted their own helmets.

Through in the cockpit, she clouted the still-dazed pilot with her forearm, slamming the woman against the fuselage's spartan lining then manhandling her clear of the exit route. She took a couple of seconds to ascertain that the officer was either dead or unconscious, and awkwardly gripped Cory's laser arm to point at the vehicle's radio controls, hoping he'd take the hint. Turned away just before the flash of brilliance.

The airlock wouldn't open. The override panel looked fried.

She turned to Cory, said 'Helmets' with as much authority as she could project, and clubbed her T-suited forearm across the reinforced C-fibre panelling of the inner hatch. Even through *steel's* analgesic haze, she felt the percussive jolt of the impact as the panelling ruptured. *That's going to leave a bruise.* Then she ripped out more of the panelling until she had pulled the latch mechanism clear of its housing. Pushed the now-misshapen hatch as far aside as it would go. The gap was only wide enough to allow her to squeeze into the airlock – Cory's ridiculously bulked-up nightsuit wouldn't fit – but, for the moment, that suited her well enough. She needed to get them clear of the crashed flarecraft before Cory's aunt had an opportunity to acquire a weapon... and before the *steel* had ebbed completely. She could feel the fade already.

The outer hatch, thankfully, was less problematic. While Titan rushed in, thick and cold, she slid the hatch aside, then turned to the task of enlarging the inner hatch opening for Cory. A few brute-force pushes widened it sufficiently. She moved to pull Cory through, and saw Teresa Maria armlocked by one of the cabin guards – Pagnell – who crazily was trying to apprehend her without having first donned a helmet. Arum fumbled at the sidearm at her hip, but Cory was quicker, reaching his right gloved hand to grip the guard's neck-flange.

Even through Arum's hastily-closed eyes, the flash was dazzling. When she opened them, Pagnell was screaming and already halfway to the cockpit's grilled floor. She made the mistake of glancing at his laserburned face as he fell...

We need to keep moving, she told herself. So that was what she did.

When she had hustled both Cory and Teresa Maria out of the vehicle and into the cavern-darkness of Titan's farside night, and had pulled them about twenty metres away from the still-gaping hatch, she signalled for them to mute comms, pressed her visor against Teresa Maria's and enunciated, loudly and clearly, 'Airworthy. Say it.' Her eyes, alert for trouble, flicked to the flarecraft canted on the dark sand, its blue and white running lights glowing uncertainly. No lights in the sky, no movement at the hatch. For now.

Good.

Cory's aunt simply stared at her, with evident malevolence.

'Say it,' Arum repeated, pausing for a sharp breath, the *steel* withdrawal already starting to bite. She struggled to ignore the dizziness, the sudden somnolence, the edging pain. 'Airworthy. So you don't die.'

'What is this?' Cory asked, nursing his arm.

'Verbal virus,' Arum explained. 'I've had it pre-prepared for months. I activated it on my helmet, it will have spread through suitcomms to all the other pharmhands by now. Your aunt too, her suit's compatible. Probably not the mil, their suits are better protected, but if Teresa Maria doesn't say the safe word, her air supply won't come back onstream.'

'So you've just asphyxiated those other... what, half-dozen pharmhands in there?'

'Look, we had to get out. We have to get moving. Teresa Maria, you need to *say it*,' Arum said. She grimaced as a jolt of pain from her arm told her that the *steel* was now well-and-truly offline; and it would be hours before the tailored infection in her thyroid had produced enough *balm* to provide some temporary relief over and above the suit's own rudimentary first aid capabilities.

Teresa Maria mumbled something that might or might not have been 'airworthy'.

'Say it again,' Arum urged. 'Don't kill yourself through failed voice recognition.'

'Airworthy,' Teresa Maria repeated, surly but with exaggerated clarity.

'Now,' Arum said, pointing back down the shallow interdune trench along which they'd flown, 'we need to get moving. Long walk back to Ponnamperuna. Cory, are you up for that, with a broken arm?'

'It's not broken, it just hurts like hell. But Ponnamperuna?' Cory gazed past the flarecraft. 'Niemann must be much closer.'

'Why do you imagine,' his aunt asked Arum, with a poisonous slowness, 'we'd go anywhere with you? After your deceit, your double-dealing led to Dayani's and Lex's deaths, and... this?'

'Teresa Maria,' Arum began. She still didn't know exactly how things had happened out by the downed CREV. There'd been scant time to read clues before the mil had showed. 'I'm sorry Dayani and Lex are dead. But it was nothing I did. And we really do not have time for this.'

'We have time,' said Teresa Maria, taking a widefooted stance. 'It will be the end of time, Arum, before I go anywhere with you. Cory?'

'I—' Cory began, then seemed to work something loose in his throat. He looked from one to the other, settled his gaze on Teresa Maria. 'Aunt Teresa's right. You did lead the pharmhands to us.'

Arum bit back a defensive distress at the coldness in his tone. 'No, Cory, I didn't. That was sheer bad luck, wrong place wrong time. You just happened to come to the zeppelin's attention, it was out hunting tonight anyway. And that, Teresa Maria, is why we're not heading for the closest settlement. The pharmhands are looking to take Niemann tonight.'

'You're *lying*,' replied Teresa Maria.

'I'm really not. And we do have to move. It won't be much longer before either the mil or the pharmhands arrive to check out this wreck. We need to be well clear when that happens. Cory?'

'Even if what you say's true,' he said, taking a few steps further from the vehicle and turning to direct a laser flash into the sand a few metres away, 'you were still collaborating with the pharmhands. You *are* a pharmhand.'

'Consider this my resignation letter,' Arum said, gesturing to the downed vehicle. She started to walk away. They'd accompany her, or they wouldn't. It was a long trek back to Ponnamperuna. And even if it hadn't been, they all still needed to put considerable distance between themselves and the flarecraft. 'Look, pharmhands aren't the villains they're painted to be. They have their own priorities, their own society, their own goals. Yes, they're militarily adventurous, they're too power-hungry for their own good, but they want this region to succeed. And look at Ponnamperuna, look at Niemann. Look at Kasprzak. Our civs are letting Sagan bleed this district dry, with all the industry moving to the elevator's shadow.'

Cory was following her. So, amazingly enough, was his aunt. 'The elevator's a done deal,' said Teresa Maria. 'The pharmhands can't change that, any more than anyone else.'

Arum activated her helmlamps. The illumination was a necessary risk. The broad valley between the long dunes was wind-smoothed, but 'smooth' didn't equate to 'flat', and they were walking away from even the flarecraft's illumination. Long shadows of uncertain depth striped the way ahead. Plus, this far into the hyperextended Titanian night, infrared could barely hint at a horizon: it couldn't sensibly provide enough insight into terrain to guide against stumbles. 'They can if the elevator's sabotaged,' she said.

'And that's their game?' Teresa Maria almost spat the question out, as though she'd never sampled anything more distasteful. 'You felt the same way?'

'I don't see that Sagan should get to hold sway, just through a fluke of geography. I still agree with them on that.'

'Most everyone round here would,' said Teresa Maria. 'But their methods—'

'Are wrong. I came to see that in time,' said Arum. 'But it's not easy to leave them, they're quite Old Testament about that. Ruthless. They have a reputation to uphold, as well as signals to send to rival gangs. I thought their goals were worthwhile, I thought their methods were just the price to pay. I thought I could help avoid, or at least reduce, bloodshed. But… it got too much. They're too fanatical, the ones in charge. This is an opportunity. I won't get another one.'

'I don't believe you,' said Cory's aunt. 'You say you wanted to avoid bloodshed, but venting the flarecraft and sabotaging the suits must've killed upwards of a half-dozen people back there. You're clearly not the mouse you played at, back in Ponnamperuna. And you talk as though you were just flirting with pharmhanding, but I saw the way you demolished the flarecraft's airlock. Pretty sure they don't provide their biotech tools to the newly-recruited. Which means I can't trust you. Which means I'm not going to follow at your heels.'

'Then why,' asked Arum, '*are* you following at my heels?'

'The mil didn't take our skid-bike, back at the hideout. Good chance it's still functional. Cory and I can use it to get to Niemann.'

'Cory, is this true?'

He didn't answer.

'You're wasting your time. The pharmhands will be lighting up Niemann within three hours. They've been planning for this for months. The mil won't know what hit them.'

'Then we'll slip in amongst the chaos,' Teresa Maria persisted.

'You'll die in the attempt. The Niemann mil are going to have you – all of us – well and truly flagged by now. And you can bet that the pharmhands will be looking to take out anyone wearing a nightsuit like Cory's.'

'We are *not going with you*,' Teresa Maria said, through what sounded like clenched teeth.

'Skid bike will only take two,' Cory noted, panting. He seemed to be struggling to keep up in the bulky nightsuit.

'Then we'll deal with that when we get to it,' said Arum. 'Won't we?'

'Company,' said Cory. Arum didn't immediately grasp his meaning, but Teresa Maria turned without hesitation back towards the downed flarecraft, now several hundred metres behind them. Following her gaze, Arum could just see traces of movement in the vehicle's airlock.

'Cory, you hot again?' Teresa Maria asked.

'Enough.'

'Then light him up.'

Cory raised his arm to the horizontal. 'Acquired.' *Flash.*

'Kill your helmlamps,' Teresa Maria said. After a couple of seconds, darkness cloaked them. After a few seconds more, the flarecraft's lights faded to black. 'Now move towards me,' she ordered, as she herself stepped a few paces away across the dune valley.

Why are we doing this? Arum asked herself. But the security specialist's advice was sound. It would be suicide to remain at a location they'd just advertised. 'He'll have night vision,' Arum protested.

'Most likely, yes. But the laser should have at least temporarily blinded him, and that rise should put us out of line of sight. For now. Arum, your gun.'

'What?'

'Someone needs to take that bastard out. So unless you know how to use that thing,' Teresa Maria said, pushing the words out as though each syllable itself were a weapon, 'give it to me.'

Arum hesitated before unlatching the sidearm. Passing it to Cory's aunt, she wondered what magnitude of mistake she was making.

Teresa Maria hefted the gun, looking at it for several seconds. Then she stepped across to Cory and awkwardly embraced his bulky suit, draping her free arm behind his neckflange. She stepped back, her torso dappled with flecks of the ice frosting that Cory's nightsuit still wore. Throughout the process, she did not make visor contact with Arum. 'Now wait here. And stay low.'

'Where are you going?'

'Gotta get closer. The range on these things isn't the best. And Cory?'

'Yes, Aunt Teresa?'

'You get hot, flash the sand, then move. I don't want to get friendly-fired, and you need to not advertise your location.' She stepped away.

Arum was surprised at how speedily Teresa Maria moved off back in the flarecraft's direction.

'Now we wait, I guess,' said Cory.

Would it complicate matters further if the aunt didn't return? Arum wondered. 'Cory, I never—'

The sound of gunfire was faint but unmistakable. Two shots, sharp, then a fade to silence. 'Are you hot enough again?' Arum asked. 'Can you see the plane in infrared? And the guard?'

'The plane, yes, but I can't... and Aunt Teresa said—'

'Aunt Teresa is likely to need all the help she can get,' Arum replied, more sharply than she'd wished. 'She's trying to tackle a mil fighter who'll have smart armour, night vision, mil-level thermal camo, and very probably automatic targeting. She's not going to get within three hundred metres before she gets picked off. So we flash up the plane's airlock, it's going to give that mil something else to worry about. But be ready to move fast.'

'Right.'

Another report, its flash like a meteor in infrared, firing somewhere off to their side. *That's heat weaponry*, she thought. Not dangerous in itself, not like the ultracompact bursts of Cory's UVA laser, but it would illuminate Teresa Maria like infrared phosphorescence, if it hit her. 'Cory, *now*.'

Cory stood, sighted. 'Acquired.' *Flash.*

'Now drop.'

More weapons fire, four or five reports, from two different directions. Starfished on the deep-chilled sand, Arum couldn't be sure which were projectiles and which were just pulsed heat.

'We need to get behind that ridge,' said Cory, rising cautiously to his knees.

'Which ridge?' Arum asked.

'North,' Cory answered. 'Amp the contrast on your IR, you should be able to make it out.'

Arum wrestled with the unfamiliar overlay on her HUD for a few seconds. 'I don't think this helmet knows that trick,' she complained.

'Then follow my voice.'

And stay low, Arum thought.

They hunkered behind the low bleb of the sand ridge for sufficiently long, just listening to the silence, not trusting themselves to speak, that she began to suspect Teresa Maria would not be returning. Arum kept hoping Cory would say something, but just as in the flarecraft's passenger cabin, he wasn't having it. Her throat prickly, she rummaged through dozens of words, rehearsing arguments, apologies, confessions; striving to find some combination that could express what she wanted to say, what she needed to say. Perhaps the right words simply didn't exist. Perhaps, tonight, Cory had been pushed just too far by circumstance. It infuriated her that there wasn't biotech for something like this. Reaction speed, pain suppression, the perception of invulnerability, even hallucinogenic escape; but not for what she truly needed most. Memories snagged in her consciousness, wasting the moments she could not claw back. Pictorial, verbal, tactile, futile. She was more alone-together with Cory than she might ever be henceforth, and she could not find the words to reach him.

All she had wanted to do was to find a way to stop the elevator. She'd messed up. And though Lex's and Dayani's deaths had not in any way been her doing, she could see how it looked.

Things had seemed so straightforward when she and Cory had been studying together, one year, two years ago, before the careers they'd been training for had been pulled out from underneath them by the all-consuming pull of Sagan and its elevator. The pharmhands had seemed a natural step at the time, committed and even more serious about training than the civ ed system had been; she'd learned a lot. But had it been of benefit?

What was there for her now? Ponnamperuna was a destination, but no safe haven. She'd have to travel much further to lose her past, and then would begin the slow process of convincing her adopted society that she possessed useful skills.

What chance that Cory would be alongside her then? Probably none. But it was a life, whatever happened.

I never wanted to deceive you. But you concealed things too…

If he marked her angst, he didn't voice it. Instead, Cory kept his own counsel. Every few minutes he canted his arm and discharged his cooling laser, aiming it discreetly in the sand some distance across from them so as to minimise the chance of giving away their precise location to anyone at or near the downed mil vehicle. There had been no further weapons fire, no indications of the skirmish's outcome. Should they backtrack to the flarecraft? But that might well be walking into a trap. Whereas to just desert Teresa Maria to an uncertain fate was never going to be palatable to Cory…

Arum was saved from a decision by the eventual sound of slow, cautious footsteps. Cory peered over the ridge before Arum could forestall him.

'Well?'

'T-suit, just one. Armed. It *looks* like Aunt Teresa, but…'

He didn't have to complete the sentence. They would have no way of knowing until it was too late. Arum felt her heart race faster. Did they have any hope of overpowering an armed mil fighter?

The steps drew closer, stopped several paces away. 'Thought I told you to fire into the sand,' the figure said, gruffly.

'Arum thought it might help.'

'Did she now.'

'Any problems?' Cory asked, standing.

'Let me get my breath,' Teresa Maria replied. She paused for several seconds, evidently as much to take a drink as to catch her breath. 'She wasn't easy to disarm.'

'Disarm?' Arum asked, sharply, pulling herself to her feet.

'I don't take a life,' said Teresa Maria acidly, 'unless I must.' Something haunted showed briefly through her visor. She tensed her face in what could have been suppression of a sneeze, before she continued, her voice strained. 'I jumped her. I couldn't kill her, in all conscience, not mil.' Another pause; she turned aside and drew a pair of deeply ragged breaths. 'She was blinded, probably the laser. The flarecraft provided just enough cover.'

'You should have offed her,' Arum muttered.

'And leave Neimann to fall to the pharmhands? Sorry, no.' Teresa Maria glanced down at the gun still gripped in her glove, and exhaled heavily. 'Her suit radio was still functional, so they'll be forewarned now, with just enough time to prepare and retaliate. Assuming that wasn't a pack of lies on your part.'

There was something deep, something implacable about Teresa Maria's hostility that Arum couldn't identify; nor did she care, particularly. She cast her gaze to the dark sand at her feet. 'It wasn't,' she replied thickly.

'We'd best be moving,' said Teresa Maria. It wasn't merely a suggestion. 'Neimann mil will have their hands too full to worry about us for a while, but that won't stay true forever.' Now, finally, she turned towards Arum. 'You needn't accompany us.'

'Is that what Cory says too?' Arum asked. 'Or just you and the gun?'

Cory chose not to respond, looked away.

'You're both carrying injuries,' Arum continued, ignoring the throbbing pain in her forearm. 'What if one of you needs support to get back to the hideout? It must be thirty, forty klicks from here. You're in no shape—'

'You might have tracking,' Teresa Maria snapped. 'I'm not taking the chance.'

'I don't,' said Arum, failing to keep the desperation out of her voice. 'And even if I did, you think I'd enable it? You honestly think I'd welcome another run-in with pharmhands, after what happened back there? Cory, are you going to let your aunt do this?'

He stared into the distance, took his time before answering. 'She did get us out of the flarecraft. We can't just leave her, Aunt Teresa.'

Teresa Maria looked from one to the other and back again, glaring at both, while something seemed to war within her. 'You can follow,' she informed Arum at last. 'But keep your distance.'

This decision made, Teresa Maria set off down the dark-shrouded dune valley, closely followed by Cory. Arum gave them a couple of minutes head start, by which time the light from their helmlamps had faded to the faintest gloaming, before she commenced her patient pursuit.

She wasn't entirely sure just when she'd ceded authority to the older woman. Had it been with the gun's handover, or on Teresa Maria's return? Whatever, there didn't seem any immediate prospect of wresting it back.

It would be almost five hours before her metabolism's microbial guests had generated sufficient *fleet* to achieve anything useful, double that or more to build up a threshold of *steel*. So, for now, all she could do was to follow behind Cory and his aunt. 'There's still only transport for two on that skid-bike,' she observed.

'We'll cross that trail,' said Teresa Maria over the suit's radio, 'when we come to it.'

We will indeed, Arum told herself.

placenta

Tiril hates the rental, but that can't be helped. At thirty-four weeks, she's not going to fit into her own suit.

The hab is bereft against the tan-scraped icescape and the tawny-hazed sky. It might once have been something, a home, a business, an outpost; it's now just a carapace. Out in the badlands – places where, admittedly, there might well be more need of emergency shelter, with settlements so sparse – a structure like this, abandoned perhaps just ten years ago, could well still be functional, or at least survivable. But this close to Sagan, where so many gather at the intersection of rebellion and disaffection – that nexus where, not too long ago, you might have found Tiril herself – there's no chance. She walks closer: the vehicle shelter's been breached, the biosystem's been gutted, even the heating panels have been ripped out. There's scrap on the ground, awaiting the slow staining that Titan visits upon every object. The hab, she can tell, is not one from which useful componentry has been salvaged as needed; no, this has been simple vandalism. Which, curiously enough, is just how Tiril likes it. There's a solemnity, an appealing mystery to the dilapidation, as the hab loses its slow battle against the two flanks of Titan and its indolently destructive inhabitants.

She'll get some good shots here.

She wishes, sometimes, that Xuan was more supportive, that he at least understood this drive of hers to catalogue the structural dissolution of abandoned sites. Her images and accompanying notes are, she maintains, significant historical documents, a perspective which he, with his blinkered geochemist's mindset, cannot seemingly acknowledge. But it can't be helped. The two of them are, otherwise – the white-lie qualifier she uses, to friends who aren't especially close, is 'in all important aspects' – a good match. Still it irks that he doesn't approve of her hobby, can't see any possible attraction. That's how it is. She's appreciative that he at least didn't make too much of an argument over her need to do this, again, *now*, while she can. While she still can. Before her world changes.

The rental, at least, is supportive, even if she doesn't like the way it smells. The exoskeleton has plenty of power; the servoes are smooth and strong; the padding holds her snugly. Her back hurts less, walking around out here in a hundred-kilo rental T-suit, than it does nowadays just pottering around their little corner of Sagan. It doesn't even force her to pee as often. She hates the suit, because it's so frustrating trying to communicate with the camera through it, but as a mobility / containment device, it could be a lot worse.

Vega's awake, and signals it with a spirited little kick just below her navel. *A southern-hemisphere kick*, Tiril thinks, unconsciously reaching a thickly-gloved hand to the suit's swollen torso. (She's been caught out by that several times today.)

It strikes her that the suit is as pregnant with her – bloated, ponderous – as she is with Vega. Keeping her warm, keeping her fed, keeping her alive.

The openings in the vehicle shelter's panelling are big enough that she should be able to enter the hab without even needing to force her way through the airlock; and enough of Titan has been into the shelter before her that she sees, quickly, a couple of good vantage points for her flavour of photography. She makes her way across the flooring cautiously, planning her route, not leaving bootmarks where she wants to shoot. She crouches down – the suit is much better at crouching, and retaining balance, than she, heavy with unfamiliar personal gravity, would be without it – and captures the scenes she wants before allowing the suit to pull her upright again. She clambers through to the hab proper.

This was a sleeping chamber, single berth. That was presumably the galley. The bathroom would most likely have been there…

Furniture, a table and a broken chair, domestic mess left strewn on the floor, to which inblown tholins have added their own unique signature. She bends, feels the rental's powerful knees lock, captures a few images in close-up then pivots so as to get the broken chair in half-silhouette against the breach in the wall. Turns again. The hab's front airlock, amazingly, is more-or-less intact. Whoever has vandalised the rest of the dwelling hasn't bothered to strip it out, hasn't even ripped out the airlock's interior control panel. Without all the plumbing, of course, it's useless, but it's the kind of detail, this unexpected remnant of functionality surrounded by decay, that she finds most appealing.

The control board even lights up, greenlights for the power and pumps, stark red for air. It's the perfect visual highlight against the surrounding room's sinking-in-sepia deterioration, and she photographs it from several angles, to ensure she gets the shots she wants.

She's in a rented suit that she both deplores and appreciates, and she's in her element.

Vega, she's determined, will appreciate the beauty of dereliction, the particularity of degradation. Or will at least be afforded the opportunity of making up her own mind, rather than simply inheriting her father's prejudices on the subject.

When she tires of finding vistas to photograph in the ruined galley – which, coincidentally, is when Vega decides to kick a bit more, sharp and solid – Tiril moves through to the sleeping chamber, to see what it offers her.

Her camera's memory replete, her photographer's mind sated, she's on her way back to the skid-bike – parked sufficiently far that it hasn't shown up in any of the exteriors – when the rental pings a problem.

A serious problem.

Tiril hopes that light on the unfamiliar helmet's HUD doesn't mean what she thinks it means.

'Suit?' she asks. 'Status?'

<*CO$_2$ scrubbing has failed, Passenger Ohanessian,*> replies the voice she hates. The rental suit's voice; not her own suit's. It doesn't sound right. <*Please hold. Rebooting now.*>

The HUD's offending red light blinks off, shines green after a few seconds; amber; red.

<*Passenger Ohanessian,*> the suit is saying, at the same time she's repeating her request for 'Status'. She's reached the skid-bike now. <*Critical failure mode; scrubbing unit is inoperative. Contacting Sagan medevac now.*>

Her heart surges, then seems to drag. *This can't be happening, not now. Not a solid two hours' drive from Sagan.* 'Medevac? How long will that take?'

<*Sagan Emergency Medical advises crisis team will reach these coordinates in thirty-four minutes. Do you wish to speak to one of Sagan Emergency Medical's advisors?*>

She takes her seat on the skid-bike's saddle, suddenly feeling all of her weight as the saddle presses her suit uncomfortably against her perineum. As if to answer it, there's a spasm, from somewhere in the base of her belly and, caught off guard, she gasps a little. Her face flushes; she can feel a sudden tiara of sweat across her brow. The contraction passes. She breathes again.

<*Passenger Ohanessian?*>

She starts the warm-up for the skid-bike's motor. Strives to ignore the small sharp shard of fear crystallising in her throat. 'How long before the CO$_2$ becomes a problem?'

<*Passenger Ohanessian, it is already a problem, and worsening. Carbon dioxide buildup in this suit will render you unconscious within seven minutes. Do you wish to speak with a Sagan EM advisor?*>

'Patch me through,' she says, looking around as if to spy, somewhere in the landscape, a miraculous solution to her sudden problem. The suit hasn't conveyed how soon death will follow after unconsciousness – perhaps it's programmed not to, out of a misguided sensibility – but it doesn't need to.

She knows thirty-four minutes for rescue is much too long.

The guilt, delayed, is almost overpowering. If she fails, Vega too will die. She feels suddenly sick at the thought. She places her gloved hand on her suit's torso, tries to steady herself.

'Tiril Ohanessian?' The voice in her earbuds is female, low-pitched, soft-spoken: a don't-scare-the-children voice.

'Speaking,' she replies, her voice pathetic, small; terrified.

'Our team is on its way, and will be with you in under thirty-three minutes. Your suit's air quality will worsen dangerously within that time, so it's vital that you secure yourself within your vehicle's passenger cabin. Are you able to access the passenger cabin?'

'It's a skidbike,' she says, with the terseness of bottled desperation.

'Oh,' says the advisor. And that single syllable, somehow conveying a sudden sense of hopelessness, is too much.

This ache in her jaw, this pressure in her eyes, those aren't tears being held back—

Vega. She's been criminally negligent; she's killed her own daughter.

As if in response, as if her unborn daughter has registered Tiril's remorse, there are three kicks in quick succession. She shifts on the saddle.

Her heart's racing. *Does that mean I'm producing CO_2 faster?*

My body, the self-poisoning machine.

'Can you operate your vehicle?' the advisor asks. 'There's a habitat just half a kilometre from your location, you should be able to take shelter—'

She terminates the connection, because she's no wish for the last voice she hears to be a stranger's. She's about to contact Xuan – to ask forgiveness, to hear his voice, to say her goodbyes – when a thought occurs to her. She fires the skid-bike into life.

<Passenger Ohanessian?>

'When I need your help,' Tiril replies, mouth set in a determination she doesn't fully feel, 'I'll ask for it. Until then, just update my location for them.'

She takes the short route, which is juddery as all hell – *I'm sorry, Vega* – and skids to an ungainly stop just metres from the ruined hab. *Here goes nothing.* Dismounting, she almost trips, and curses herself for the delay.

The airlock's exterior control panel has been vandalised. She swears, loses precious seconds stumbling on her way around to the vehicle shelter, fits herself through the largest rent in the wall. Her eyes will take too long to adapt to the shelter's low light levels, so she calls up her helmet's lights, buttery and warm. She's already feeling drowsy, forgets for a moment what she's looking for in the shelter. Clambers through the breach between two panels, into the ruined sleeping chamber. Stands. Takes stock. Moves through into the galley.

Oxygen isn't a problem: her suit has plenty, an hour's worth even without the scrubber's replenishment. What will kill her, what will kill Vega, is the carbon dioxide buildup.

She steps around the table, tries to read the pictograms on the airlock's control board. Her eyes feel blurry, bleary, so she wipes her visor… which makes it worse. *Think*, she commands herself, trying to reconstruct in her mind the sequence that, a minute ago, she thought she had fixed in her memory. This would be so much simpler, if everything wasn't so tiring.

Got to focus.

She presses the 'open' pictogram, and the airlock's inner hatch obligingly slides open. She steps into the boothlike interior.

The airlock's central control panel, within the airlock itself, has been vandalised, perhaps by the same person who ripped out the lock's outer controls. *Shit.*

She steps back into the galley, stares at the working control board again. *Head so heavy. Open… close… but I need… I need…* 'Suit?' she asks.

<*Passenger Ohanessian?*>

'I need to know how to set a delayed hatch closure on this airlock, and a two-minute pumping cycle. Open, ten seconds, close, evacuate, two minutes, stop. Can you do this? Priority?'

<*Please wait*,> the suit says. Seconds pass. Each increment of forced inactivity is like an invitation to nap.

She bites her lip.

The suit instructs her on the sequence of keypresses to effect the operation she's after.

It wouldn't kill the suit to speak a little faster.

She's having more trouble, every few seconds, staying focussed. Feigning even the semblance of alertness. Sleep, the idea of sleep, has become something seductive; vertiginous; unquenchable. Her gloved fingertips are knobs of wood.

Will the suit tell her if she has mispressed the sequence?

The airlock hatch opens, she stares at it for a few seconds before remembering that she's to step inside, even if, for now, she can't remember exactly why. She steps inside. The hatch slides closed behind her, and she's in the booth.

Which floor did she want? She forgets.

There's a roar, and the suit's exoskeleton strains against decompression, as the atmosphere within the airlock, chilled and poisonous, is pumped away. The change in the feel of the suit's confinement around her invigorates Tiril, briefly, and may even have transmitted itself through to Vega, judging by a spot of bumping around in there. *Movement is good*, Tiril thinks. *Just don't ring the doorbell yet, kid.*

She turns on the spot, to face the inner hatch; a task which requires increased effort from her, because the suit's servoes, designed to function smoothly against Titan's one-and-a-half atmospheres, don't work as well in the unaccustomed vacuum.

Two minutes is an eternity... She dreams. The roar of the sea, wings, a tiger. She's curious as to what's keeping her aloft: it's herself.

She's awoken by an increasingly loud chime within her helmet. *<Passenger Ohanessian. Passenger Ohanessian,>* intones a voice behind the chime.

Reality returns. *The airlock.* She reaches up to manipulate the quick-release on her helmet's neck flange, but her fingers aren't working properly. She's just scrabbling. *The gloves' servoes must be struggling in the vacuum also.* And she remembers what needs to happen next.

'Suit?' she asks, her voice sleep-thick.

<Passenger Ohanessian?>

'I need air out there. Please vent.'

<You are asking me to release breathable air into an evacuated chamber contaminated by low-volatility atmospheric constituents?>

She has to think through this, muddleheadedly unravelling it to be sure it's not some kind of verbal trap. *So tired...* 'You have enough reserves for that? For one standard atmosphere's pressure?'

<Ample,> says the suit. *<But—>*

She cuts it short, before the enveloping dullness can confuse her again. 'Yes. Do it.'

There's a hiss, from somewhere above her suit's backtank. It sounds like the world's longest intake of breath, sharp and sustained, though it is in truth more of an exhalation, of course. And now she must wait, because even the three-cubic-metres space of the airlock takes time to fill. *Sleepy.*

It's a good thing, she realises belatedly, that she didn't succeed in working the quick-release earlier. With the airlock pumped to vacuum, her helmet might well have cracked on the airlock ceiling – or the ceiling itself might have shattered. Not to mention the effects on her body of sudden decompression...

'External pressure?' she asks the suit.

<Point five four,> it announces, *<and rising. But Passenger Ohanessian, I am concerned at the temperature, which is dramatically below human-optimal.>*

'I'll manage,' she says, yawning. 'Alarm me when it gets to point nine five atmospheres.'

She's working her fingers in syrup, drifting from one fugue state to the next while the noise around her head whines with noise overlaid upon something which, in another life, she might have recognised as words. Soon be over now. *Soft bed, sleep—*

There was something she had needed to do... what was it? She had to lift off her head, because it wasn't working, and when your head stops working it's time to get another...

The helmet. Her heart is striving to thump, her eyes, burning dry, are trying to not stay closed…

She reaches up, first with one hand, then the other, then both; and pulls her helmet off, scraping her nose on the neck-flange. The pain – part abrasion, part sudden frozen-dessert headache – focusses her as she gingerly lifts the helmet clear, breathes air that's unbelievably cold and dead-smelling… the cold helps. She takes a long breath, another, trying to clear her lungs of the backload of carbon dioxide. Her breath fogs the air. *Mama dragon*, she thinks, and smiles at the notion. Then grimaces: the headache has sharpened, intensified, settled in.

'Suit?' she asks, though the air is now so cold it's painful to talk. 'Time until the Sagan paramedics get here?'

< *Twenty-six minutes,*> it informs her. She feels dispirited – twenty-six minutes still seems an eternity – but she thinks the expanded air supply will slow the carbon dioxide buildup enough to keep her – and Vega – alive that long. It's going to be cold, though. She's about to demand that the suit turn up its heating when she sees something that gives her pause.

There's frost forming on the airlock's walls.

Part of the frost, she knows, will be water ice, frozen out from the moisture of her breath, and from the suit's stale air. But with the airlock sitting at an ambient temperature around a hundred degrees below the freezing point of carbon dioxide, a fair proportion of it must be dry ice.

The airlock is cold enough that it is trapping out the thing which would have killed her. The ultracold walls, right now, are what is keeping her alive.

It's filtering out the toxins, she thinks, delightedly. *Vega, your Mum is cleverer than she knew.*

Vega kicks in response, though it's not clear whether she's agreeing with her mother, or disagreeing, or simply registering another complaint regarding the circumstances of her ongoing tenancy. Really, it doesn't matter which.

The next twenty-six minutes, nonetheless, are the longest of both their lives.

Small presses depend on word of mouth.

If you've enjoyed this book, please mention it to friends.
Or leave a review on Goodreads, Amazon, LibraryThing, or elsewhere.

acknowledgements

'Storm in a T-Suit' was first published in *Aurealis* 44 (2010), ed. Stuart Mayne. 'Broadwing' was first published in *Tales for Canterbury* (Random Static: eds Cassie Hart & Anna Caro, 2011). 'Hatchway' was first published in *Anywhere But Earth* (coeur de lion: ed. Keith Stevenson, 2011). 'Emptying Roesler' was first published in *Regeneration* (Random Static: eds Anna Caro & Juliet Buchanan, 2013). 'CREVjack' and 'Fixing a Hole' were first published in *Difficult Second Album: more stories of Xenobiology, Space Elevators, and Bats Out Of Hell* (Peggy Bright Books: ed. Edwina Harvey, 2014). 'Lakeside' was first published as 'Lakeside on the Via Australis' in *Perihelion SF* (Oct. 2014), ed. Sam Bellotto Jr. 'Erebor', 'Goldilock', 'Phlashback', and 'Placenta' are new to this collection.

about the author

Born and raised in North Canterbury, New Zealand, Simon Petrie now lives in Canberra, Australia, with his books, his occasional ongoing forays into scientific research, and his least-effort plans for galactic domination. His short fiction has appeared in numerous places; much of it has been conveniently corralled into the new short fiction collection *80,000 Totally Secure Passwords That No Hacker Would Ever Guess* (released Oct. 2018). He has been shortlisted several times for the Sir Julius Vogel, Ditmar, and Aurealis Awards, and he has won the Sir Julius Vogel Award three times: in 2010 for Best New Talent and in 2013 and 2018, with *Flight 404* and *Matters Arising from the Identification of the Body* respectively, for Best Novella. He also scored a coveted Dishonourable Mention in the 2011 Bulwer-Lytton Fiction Contest.

He has edited five issues (numbers 35, 40, 51, 54, and 61) of *Andromeda Spaceways Inflight Magazine*, and has co-edited two anthologies (*Light Touch Paper, Stand Clear* and *Use Only As Directed*, published by Peggy Bright Books) with Edwina Harvey and one (*Next*, published by CSFG Publishing) with Rob Porteous. He's also acted as a typesetter and e-book formatter for several small-press and indie publishers in Australia and North America. He is currently a member of the Canberra Speculative Fiction Guild and SpecFicNZ writers' communities.

want more titan fiction?

She took her helmet off.
That's where it starts; that's where it ends.
That's all there is.

Tanja Morgenstein, daughter of a wealthy industrialist and a geochemist, is dead from exposure to Titan's lethal, chilled atmosphere, and Guerline Scarfe must determine why.

This novella blends hard-SF extrapolation with elements of contemporary crime fiction, to envisage a future human society in a hostile environment, in which a young woman's worst enemies may be those around her.

Simon Petrie's *Matters Arising from the Identification of the Body* is a Sir Julius Vogel Award winning SF / mystery novella, out now.

www.ingramcontent.com/pod-product-compliance
Lightning Source LLC
Chambersburg PA
CBHW021429110726
47901CB00008B/2358